Maa⋯   for
Lee   his
boyh⋯   ⋯re
who   It
mean⋯   ⋯m
Trac⋯   ad
marr⋯   ⋯cy
hated   ⋯ee
Trac⋯   in
which   ad
taken   ad
seen   d.
Two   to
dull t⋯   ⋯e
sixgu⋯   ⋯t
it ha⋯   ⋯w
he w⋯   ⋯d
he w⋯

SMOKY PASS

L. P. Holmes

CURLEY LARGE PRINT
HAMPTON, NEW HAMPSHIRE

Library of Congress Cataloging-in-Publication Data

Holmes, L. P. (Llewellyn Perry), 1895–
    Smoky pass / L. P. Holmes.
    p. (large print) cm.
    ISBN 0–7927–1966–2.—ISBN 0–7927–1965–4 (pbk.)
    1. Large type books.   I. Title.
[PS3515.04448S63   1994]   93–42873
813'.52—dc20   CIP

British Library Cataloguing in Publication Data available

This Large Print edition is published by Chivers Press, England, and by Curley Large Print, an imprint of Chivers North America, 1993.

Published by arrangement with the Golden West Literary Agency in association with Laurence Pollinger Ltd.

U.K. Hardcover ISBN 0 7451 2163 2
U.K. Softcover   ISBN 0 7451 2175 6
U.S. Hardcover   ISBN 0 7927 1966 2
U.S. Softcover   ISBN 0 7927 1965 4

Printed in Great Britain

CHAPTER ONE

They were a full four days out of Comanche Junction, and here, finally, the last of the desert's bitter miles lay behind them. For the past thirty hours there had been little water for themselves and none at all for the horse herd or the saddle mounts. Now this day was ending, drowning the desert in hot, blue shadow and darkening the first lift of the Mingo Hills ahead.

A dry wash slashed the slope at a northerly angle and into it the horse herd poured, swinging wildly back and forth in search of the water that had once flowed over this parched, alkali-scabbed gravel.

Ben Pardee's heavy yell sailed across the dusk.

'Push 'em—push 'em! Get 'em out of there!'

The far side of the wash was high and steep, a sandy bank which sloughed and slid and gave way under scrambling hoofs, filling the air with a boil of dust. In the thick of it, Lee Tracy twice had his mount near knocked from under him by the buffeting charges of water-desperate animals, so frantic and feverish was their milling. Off to his right he caught the echo of Jack Dhu's high-pitched Texas squawl, and to his left, Mack

1

Driscoll's whoop.

Thus contained, the horses, trampling and crowding, were ready to break back the way they had come, but this move Tracy managed to block with a swinging riata end and his own dust-clotted shouts. One of the horses, with wild, lunging effort, finally won a way up that far bank, breaking a rift through which others followed. So, presently, the wash was empty. Beyond it the horse herd, drained and weary, slowed to an uneasy halt.

Lee Tracy spat, scrubbed a hand across lips made rough by sun and dust and stinging alkali, then spat again. He shucked the makings of a smoke from his shirt pocket, sprinkling Durham from a thinning sack into a somewhat crumpled trough of brown paper, then twisted in his saddle and handed over the muslin sack of tobacco as Jack Dhu's drawl sounded.

'I could use a little of that.'

They had their cigarettes rolled and alight when Ben Pardee and Mack Driscoll came up. Pardee threw his usual blunt growl.

'That the best crossing you could find? I could have left some crippled horses in that damn wash.'

Tracy fought back a tired anger and kept his answer even.

'Been two years since I was by this way, and since then the wash has been storm-cut.'

With quickening feeling he added, 'I never promised to show you anything, Pardee, except the shortest way across the desert to Smoky Pass, which is dead ahead. I'll say one more thing, then keep my mouth shut. If the horses were mine they'd stay right here until tomorrow morning.'

'Tomorrow morning!' blurted Pardee. 'You mean spend another night in this damned desert? What kind of a fool idea are you trying to sell?'

'No fool idea at all. It's like this. At night a wind blows out of Maacama Basin into the desert. It really rips through the pass and it's heavy with the smell of the river. The horses get a sniff of that, they could break wild for the water. They do, we'll never hold them, and in the dark they'll scatter to hell and gone. They get too much water, too quick, some might even founder. I knew of an outfit that brought some cattle through the pass from this side after dark, and they lost plenty, just that way.'

Ben Pardee waved an impatient arm.

'You're trying to build an empty scare, Tracy. If the broncs run, we can hold them.'

Tracy shrugged, said nothing further. He might have known it would be useless to argue. He had hired on with Pardee at Comanche Junction, and regretted the fact after the first day and night in the desert. For Pardee had turned out to be overbearing and

3

stubborn, as weighty of tongue and manner as he was physically burly.

Jack Dhu sucked deeply on his cigarette and offered a brief opinion.

'Might pay to listen, Pardee. Tracy knows this country. You and me and Driscoll don't.'

Mack Driscoll, a cautious one, said nothing, his broad cheeks showing no expression in the brief flare of the match which he nursed alight and touched to the end of his smoke.

Ben Pardee settled the matter by repeating himself.

'The broncs run, we can hold them. We go on through!'

Day slipped away completely as they finished their smokes. West, across the dark gulf of the desert, the sunset sky cooled into grayness and the evening star began a first faint winking. Tracy stepped from his saddle, driving his boot heels solidly against the earth to break up the riding stiffness that had locked his back and hips and given a stumpy feeling to his legs.

Afoot and erect, he stood a full inch over six feet, with a rider's supple waist and spare flanks. His shoulders carried good width and his chest was deep and solid. Swiftly he freed the latigo, let the cinch swing, then lifted saddle and blanket from his mount. Gathering several handfuls of scanty foliage

4

from the stunted sagebrush round about, he vigorously scrubbed down that sweat-caked back, an act of consideration which won an appreciative hide-loosening shake by the horse, and the swing of a nuzzling head. He reversed the saddle blanket, replaced the saddle, caught up the cinch, looped and tightened the latigo.

As he went back into the saddle, Ben Pardee grunted scoffingly.

'What good did that do?'

'Maybe none,' answered Tracy shortly. 'But I like to think it meant something to a tired bronc.'

Pardee laughed, short and sarcastic. 'Then you better get up at point and lead out.'

So they went on, with Jack Dhu and Pardee and Mack Driscoll working the flanks and the drag. As the upward pitch of the hill slope quickened, Tracy looked back across his shoulder and saw the horse herd as a dark and shifting blur. Only by an occasional urging shout could he locate Jack Dhu and the others.

Calling on past knowledge of these hills and judging by the present pace, he figured Smoky Pass about an hour ahead, and he settled back to ride both time and distance out stoically. Weariness was a dragging weight all through him. Hunger pinched him, and in turn was dulled by the insistent misery of thirst.

He lifted the canteen high, draining what was left in it—a single frugal mouthful of tepid, alkali-bitter moisture. It did little good except to slightly lessen the thickness of his tongue.

Ahead, the slope climbed steadily, toward a velvet sky now strewn with brightening stars. Air moved against the whisker roughness of his cheek and he swung his head warily. But soon he eased against the cantle again. For this vagrant stir of air carried no hint of moisture; instead only the dry, punishing remnants of the day's desert heat, still drifting along the hill flank.

In a mood but little less than somber, Tracy recalled the last time he had traveled this west slope of the Mingo Hills. Two years ago it had been and then he was heading away from Maacama Basin instead of toward it. Two full years that had been anything but pleasant ones. For he had found that no matter how fast or far a man might ride, it was never fast or far enough to get completely away from the past and its memories.

Memories of Lucy Garland. No, that wasn't quite right, either. He had to quit thinking of her as Lucy Garland, but instead as Mrs Tasker Scott. And what a lot of fine, great dreams had been shot all to hell by that fact!

Like on that fateful evening when he'd

ridden over to Hack Garland's Lazy Dollar headquarters, and found the three of them standing on the ranchhouse porch. Hack Garland, Lucy, and Tasker Scott. With Lucy and Tasker all dressed up. Hack Garland had wasted no time in bluntly giving out the word. Lucy and Tasker Scott had been married that afternoon.

Totally unexpected and seasoned with malice, it was as brutal as a blow in the face. For Hack, full of strong ideas of power and money, had never looked with approval on any romantic affair between his daughter and such as Lee Tracy, who was just a junior partner of Buck Theodore, and Buck's Flat T holdings were on the modest side.

While Hack Garland gave out the shattering word, Tasker Scott had smiled his cold and mocking triumph. Had Lucy shown any sign of regret or remorse, or gentleness of any kind, it might have helped a little. But she had stood serene in her dark and sultry beauty, apparently quite uncaring, and the entire affair left Tracy so sick inside he could think of nothing save the wild desire to get away—as far away as possible.

He had almost ridden his horse into the ground, getting back to home headquarters. There, while packing his warbag and catching up a fresh horse, he briefly gave Buck Theodore the word. Good old Buck had made no attempt to hold him back, but

7

instead seemed to understand. So that night Lee Tracy rode out through Smoky Pass, vowing to leave Maacama Basin forever.

Which was just a fallacy inspired by hurt and disillusionment. Forever, Tracy had found, measured out as a long time—a very long time! And time could do things to a man. It could heal hurts that had once seemed mortal. It could season him and toughen him and bring him back to sound balance and the understanding of true values. Also to recognition of an obligation due Buck Theodore.

Decision to return to Maacama Basin had been just as abruptly arrived at as had been the one to leave, and it came to him while he lay in his blankets in the bunkhouse of Boley Jackson's Line J headquarters on the Skull Mountain range. One moment he'd been a tired saddle hand, about to doze off. The next he was a bundle of urgency, scarce able to wait until morning to be on his way. Which hadn't exactly made good sense, but that was the way it was.

Now, there ahead, the shoulders of Smoky Pass were beginning to loom against the stars, and beyond lay Maacama Basin.

This crossing through the Mingo Hills was neither particularly lofty, nor the approach to it overly steep or abrupt. So, presently, the upward climb softened into a gradual leveling which indicated the beginnings of the gut of the pass. And only here did the walls draw in enough to suggest any feeling of confinement.

Met by the first hint of cooling air, Tracy swung restless shoulders and twisted in his saddle for another look at the dark, shifting pack of horseflesh behind him. While overhead, a faint, almost eerie sighing began.

This was the night wind from Maacama Basin, its voice, its touch. At the moment it was flowing along the higher reaches of the pass walls, but Tracy knew that not too much further along, where the eastern down-slope began there it would be rushing close to the earth, carrying the message of the river to questing, water-famished equine nostrils.

What could happen then, only the gods might guess.

One thing, Tracy decided tiredly, was certain. When Ben Pardee refused flatly to heed his warning of possible consequences in taking the horse herd through the pass at night, he himself was freed of any further real responsibility. All he had agreed to do when hiring on with Pardee at Comanche Junction, he had done, and his warning about the pass had been made in entire good faith. So now, if the horses did run, the only sensible concern would be for the safety of his own neck.

Under him, his mount was wearing down.

He could tell this by the effort the animal put into every laboring stride. It had been a rough, tough haul on both men and horses across the desert at this dry season of the year.

Another surge of air met Tracy and this one was cool and water-scented. It lifted him high and alert in his saddle. Here and now was the point of danger. Here the horse herd would or would not react. Here, if it was going to run, it would run. He almost held his breath, waiting for the answer. And the answer came—and there was no mistaking it.

It began as a shrill, gusty snorting, laced with wildness. It was a sound to raise the hair at the nape of a man's neck. Ominous as it was, it was quickly drowned out by one far more so—the roll of running hoofs that quickly became an explosive, battering roar on the rocky bed of the pass.

Understanding all too well how small the hope of holding back any part of this surge of elemental frenzy whirling down on him from the dark, still Tracy made an attempt, yelling and swinging the hard coils of his riata.

It was a twig trying to hold back a tempest, a pebble to hold back an avalanche. He was caught up and swept along, and, knowing what it would mean to go down before those wildly charging hoofs, he gave his horse its head and dug in the spurs. And from somewhere the animal drew on enough strength to race down slope ahead of the frenzied tide.

Tracy's first thought was that he might angle away and thus break into the clear at one of the flanks of the charging herd. He quickly realized this couldn't be done; he had neither the speed nor the necessary time. There was nothing to do but drive straight ahead, hoping grimly that his horse would not stumble, and gamble that when the river flats were reached, the herd would break and scatter enough to leave a man clear of danger.

Beyond the eastern approach of the pass, the down sweep of the slope became a curving swale which angled sharply before losing itself in the river flats. Running full out, the horse herd went down the swale like a torrent of water, rapidly shortening the distance to the river and sweeping everything before it. And it was as he swung through the final sharp angle of the swale, riding desperately, that Lee Tracy saw the ruddy glow of the campfire, dead ahead.

He saw other things. There was the dark loom of a heavy wagon on one fringe of the firelight, and the pale lift of a tent off to the other side. He saw human figures dodging away from the fire toward the safety of the wagon's bulk, and he heard a man's call lift high and frantic above the tumult of the charging horse herd.

11

'Kip! Kip—'

Movement broke from the tent, a slim, darting feminine figure at the outermost reach of the firelight's thin radiance. Her dress fluttered about her as she ran, and fair hair flowed over her shoulders. A glance told that she'd never make the shelter of the wagon in time. She'd be caught in that short interval of open and smashed down—trampled.

Tracy hauled at the reins, drove straight at her, hauled at the reins again, setting his horse up in a sliding, spinning, half-stop, just short of her. He leaned far out, reaching with the circle of his right arm. He shouted.

'Grab! Grab at me!'

She had courage, this girl, and a quickness of mind to go with it. For she threw herself upward, her hands catching at his shoulders. Tracy had only time to haul her in against his hip when frantic, thundering horseflesh crashed into them.

The impact drove them yards ahead, wildly struggling yards, when it seemed, for one bleak, heart-stopping moment, that they surely must go down—horse, rider, and this slim, clinging girl. In fact, they did go partially down. Then, fighting gallantly, the horse somehow found its feet again, and plunging madly, broke into the small, clear eddy of safety in the lee of the wagon. For, like water splitting on a rock, the horse herd, as the big wagon loomed in its way, raced past either end of the rig and belted a mad way on to the river.

The fire and the tent offered no like areas of safety. One animal, slowed by the flames in front of it, was driven skidding through by its onrushing fellows, scattering coals and embers, which were in turn swiftly trampled to nothingness. The tent, no obstacle at all, was beaten down, torn and shredded in an instant.

A horse struck the low, extended tongue of the wagon, turned completely over and came down with smashing fall. It lay as it fell, head twisted under. Another animal, tripping over the same obstacle, went down, rolled, regained its feet and blundered on, a front leg loose and swinging. Shortly after, the last straggler of the herd was past and the night lay numbed and breathless.

Figures crawled from under the wagon and a woman's voice called, shrill with strain and fright.

'Kip! Kip, child—'

'I'm all right, Mother.'

The voice was slightly husky and with only the barest touch of tremor in it, and was so close to Lee Tracy's ear he could feel the faint beat of her breath. Her next words were for him.

'You—hold me so tight—I can hardly breathe—'

He loosed the tautness of his arm and she slid away from him to the ground. He answered gruffly.

'I had to make sure I didn't drop you.'

A childish whimpering sounded by the wagon and again came the woman's strained worry.

'Kip—you're sure?'

'Yes, Mother—quite sure. I'm all right.'

Tracy stepped from his saddle on to legs that were rubbery. It had been a close thing, a very close thing, and the reaction now held him fully. A truculent, angry man came out of the dark.

'What the hell's the idea, running horses wild through a man's camp? You might have killed the lot of us!'

Tracy let out a long, slow breath.

'Friend, I was more scared than you folks. Sorry, of course. It was one of those things. The horses were brought in across the desert and were crazy for water. Coming through the pass they got the breath of the river and they broke and ran for it. Your camp happened to be in their way.'

'Why shouldn't it be here?' came the harsh retort. 'This is my land. I settled on it. I got a right to set up camp!'

'Dad—please!' It was the girl. 'This rider had no way of knowing we'd be here. Instead of blaming him, we should thank him for hauling me to safety.' Her hand fell on

14

Tracy's arm. 'I do thank you, greatly.'

'The luck,' he told her simply, 'broke good for both of us.'

Came the pound of more hoofs, speeding down the slope. Out ahead carried Ben Pardee's heavy shout.

'Tracy! Where the hell are you? Tracy!'

Tracy moved past the end of the wagon and sent his answer.

'Over here!'

They came spurring up; Pardee, Jack Dhu and Mack Driscoll. They pulled in by the dark loom of the wagon and Pardee's voice ran profane and wild.

'Why ain't you with the horses? Damned if I don't believe—!'

'Cut it fine, Pardee, cut it fine!' Tracy hit back at him curtly. 'The horses stampeded right through this camp and we're in big luck that nobody was trampled.'

'Hell with the camp!' stormed Pardee. 'Only a fool granger would be dumb enough to set up a camp right under a pass.'

'And only a bigger fool would bring a horse herd through that pass at night, after the desert crossing,' retorted the man of the camp. 'The animals were sure to break for water.'

'Which he was told,' put in Jack Dhu surprisingly.

'You own those horses?' demanded the granger of Pardee.

15

'If I do,' blustered Pardee, 'what about it?'

'This about it. You've caused me damage and I expect you to make it good. I'm John Vail. What's your name?'

In the short silence that fell, Lee Tracy could sense sly retreat by Ben Pardee. Mention of a damage claim stilled some of his arrogant bluster. Tracy's accumulated dislike deepened to contempt. As he went back into his saddle he spoke up clearly.

'You must have missed it when I named him before, friend. It's Pardee, Ben Pardee. Me, I'm Lee Tracy.'

This, he thought, must surely set Pardee off again. But he didn't care, for he was about done with Ben Pardee. Yet it wasn't Pardee who spoke up. It was Jack Dhu, making blunt pronouncement again.

'It's your own fault, Pardee. You were warned. Tracy told you what could happen if you drove through the pass at night. Well, it's happened. And if it costs you money, it's your hard luck.'

Again Tracy expected violent reaction by Pardee. None came, suggesting that Pardee did not have the nerve to face up to lank, cold-jawed Jack Dhu. The best Pardee could manage was an evasive grumble.

'I got no money on me now. Won't have until I collect for the horses.'

Tracy turned to John Vail. 'How much would you say was due you?'

16

The wagon man was silent while he figured for a moment. 'The tent cost thirty dollars and was new. There was some women's gear in it, which I doubt is much use now. I'll call it square for fifty dollars.'

'That,' stated Jack Dhu flatly, 'is more than fair. How about it, Pardee? Better pay the man.'

'I tell you, I ain't got that much money on me now,' mumbled Pardee sulkily. 'When I'm paid off, I'll be back this way. Now there's a big chore ahead, locating those horses and bunching them again. Let's beat it. Come on, Tracy!'

Pardee reined away, Jack Dhu and Mack Driscoll following. Lee Tracy lingered a moment.

His glance searched the dark about him, a dark not quite so deep as it had been, for now the massing stars were beginning to flood the world with a silver radiance. He could see these people fairly clearly, the older woman with two frightened youngsters clinging to her skirts, the man, square framed and sturdy, and the girl with that rich, husky voice and fair hair reflecting the star shine.

'When he's paid off for his horses, he said,' remarked John Vail doubtfully. 'That could be a long time from now, where my claim is concerned. I doubt I'll ever see the fellow again—him or his money, either.'

17

Lee Tracy built a smoke, scratched a match across his saddle skirt, cupped it in his hands while it cooked off the sulphur and grew to full glow, then tipped his head to meet it, the brief, tiny bomb of light picking out his features in lean, hard bronze. He scuffed out the match and spoke quietly.

'I'll remind him. I'm mighty glad nobody got hurt.'

The night claimed him. The girl by the wagon stood watching while horse and rider melted into the star-glow. After which she listened until the sound of hoofs had vanished, too.

John Vail was still skeptical. 'I'm not counting on that money. I don't trust saddle hands—not any of them.'

'That's not fair, John,' remonstrated his wife. 'We're deeply in the debt to one of them, at least. Kip, dear, how he got you clear, I'll never know.'

The girl smiled softly to herself.

'I know, Mother. I know!'

CHAPTER TWO

The last time Lee Tracy had been in Antelope, it had been a small, sleepy place with a run of weathered buildings scattered along either side of a short, dusty street.

18

That had been two full years ago.

Now the town was three times as big and still growing. The main street reached well out and had a cross street bisecting it. Added structures lifted on all sides, advertising their newness with walls of raw lumber. More of the same were going up, the clatter of hammers and the whine of saws spreading steady echoes along a street stridently active with a tide of wagons and a flow of people.

It was early afternoon. Under the overhang of Asa Bingham's store porch, weary from an all-night and all-morning siege of driving activity, Lee Tracy and Jack Dhu squatted on their heels and dozed in the welcome shade. Mack Driscoll had been with them for a while, but had drifted away on some business of his own.

It had taken up to within an hour of the present moment to locate and bunch the survivors of Ben Pardee's run-away horse herd and bring them on to a newly built cluster of corrals at the edge of town. Now Pardee was off to see the man who had contracted for delivery of the horses. After which, Pardee was to return and settle up for wages owed.

Presently Jack Dhu stirred, scrubbed restless shoulders against the wall at his back and made drawling comment.

'Pardee don't show pretty quick, I go find him. I need food under my belt and a few

19

dollars in my jeans to make me feel like a human being again.'

Tracy smiled faintly. 'Does that suggest you don't entirely trust friend Pardee?'

Jack Dhu spat and again rubbed his shoulders against the wall.

'Not any,' he admitted pungently. 'In my time I've met a few men I'd trust with my shirt. Ben Pardee ain't one of them. I've seen too many of the bully-puss kind like him turn shifty, should they think they can get away with it. I'll feel some better when I get my wages safe in my pocket.'

'That granger, John Vail,' murmured Tracy, 'he'll feel better once he has his damage money.'

Jack Dhu grunted. 'I'd hate to have a leg bet that he gets it. That was a damn close call those folks had. The girl, if she don't mention you in her prayers, she ought to.'

Tracy's musing smile lingered, his thoughts casting back. He was finding it almost difficult to accept some of the past night's happenings as reality. So many things had happened so fast with a need so desperate. And with his own reactions so nearly instinctive, automatic, with no move directly dictated by ordered thought.

Remaining clearest, of course, were the high spots. Like the exultation he'd known when he held the girl secure in the circle of his arm. Then the desperate fear when it

20

seemed his horse must surely go down under the shock of wild collision. And finally, when full safety had been won in the sheltering lee of the wagon, the relief that had left him rubbery-legged and shaking-weak.

Fully remembered, too, was the husky sweetness of the girl's voice when she thanked him, and the way the star-shine seemed to build a glow about her fair head.

Kip, her folks had called her. Kip Vail!

Jack Dhu's drawl filtered through Tracy's preoccupation.

'Maybe we did Mister Pardee wrong. For here comes payday. Wonder who his fancy friend is? Looks kinda like a tin-horn to me.'

Tracy lifted his head, looked, and went still. Ben Pardee was approaching at a long angle across the street. With him was a big, fleshy, floridly handsome man wearing a tall, expensive, cream colored Stetson. The rest of the apparel was in keeping: a tan silk shirt and smoothly knotted brown tie, whipcord trousers and hand-stitched half-boots.

Tracy spoke softly. 'Not that it means anything to you, Jack. But you are gazing at Mister Tasker Scott.'

Jack Dhu swung a lean head. 'Strong on the "Mister", eh?'

'Oh, very!' nodded Tracy dryly.

Pardee and his companion dodged a ramshackle spring wagon, gained the store porch and came along it. Pardee waved an indicating hand.

'Judge for yourself,' he said to the man with him. 'I don't know enough about either of them to go down the line for them.'

Jack Dhu was quickly on his feet, openly antagonistic.

'Just what in hell is this?' he demanded coldly. 'An auction, maybe? You're talking of men, Pardee, not horses!'

Ben Pardee colored angrily under the bite of the words.

'Mr Scott is looking for some saddle hands.'

'He's not looking at me,' retorted Jack Dhu. 'For I'm not interested in anything except what you owe me. And for that I've waited long enough. So—pay me!'

Tasker Scott had said no word. He was staring at Lee Tracy, all hint of affability fading from his face, his slightly protuberant eyes turning as hard and glinting as brown bottle glass. Tracy pushed erect, showing a small, mirthless grin.

'Surprise, eh Tasker? Probably figured you'd seen the last of me. Well, it's a big world, so it is. Yet trails have a way of circling back.' He looked Scott up and down with a survey purely sardonic. 'You seem to have prospered, Tasker. Must be that Hack Garland is treating his son-in-law very well. For you're growing a paunch.'

Tasker Scott's lips pulled tight and the

22

floridness in his well-fed cheeks deepened. He came around on Ben Pardee angrily.

'Why didn't you tell me this fellow Tracy was one of your men?'

Startled, Pardee floundered a little. 'I—well—hell, how was I to know you had met him before? All I knew about him was that he'd once been in Maacama Basin and could show me the short way across the desert from Comanche Junction. So, I hired him on.'

Scott returned his fuming glance to Tracy, then made harsh remark.

'You made a mistake in coming back, Tracy.'

Tracy's grin grew openly mocking. 'Maybe—maybe not. Who can say for sure? Anyway, now that I'm here I aim to stay a while and renew old acquaintances.'

Tasker Scott rolled up on his toes and for a moment it seemed he was about to launch himself physically at Tracy. Then he turned and plunged away, his boot heels rapping hard and sharp on the worn planks of the store porch. Jack Dhu showed Tracy a pair of raised eyebrows.

'I don't believe that fellow likes you. He acts as if you'd just slid a knife into him—and twisted it.'

'Maybe I did,' Tracy admitted. 'Good old Tasker! Does me good to see him squirm.'

Jack Dhu turned to Ben Pardee, held out

his hand.

'Well?'

Pardee pulled a wad of currency from a hip pocket and peeled off several bills. Jack Dhu took them, counted them, then observed caustically.

'You got more than enough left to square up with that granger, Pardee.'

Pardee shrugged sulkily. 'Hell with him! You think I'm sucker enough to let a damn whining granger gouge me? Not a chance! Let him whistle.'

Pardee pocketed the balance of his money and started to turn away. Tracy caught him by the arm.

'Forgetting something aren't you, Pardee?'

Pardee came back at him with a show of belligerence.

'Not forgetting a damn thing. Like putting you up at point last night to keep my horses under control coming through the pass. Instead of doing it, you lost your nerve and let them run. And I lost four of the best. Two with broken legs, and had to be shot. Another foundered in the river. The fourth broke its neck falling over the tongue of that granger wagon. When I add up what those broncs were worth, I figure I don't owe you a cent.'

Lee Tracy blinked, not quite sure he was hearing right. Did this fellow actually think he could get away with anything so raw?

Surely he was joking, and with slow distinctness, Tracy said so.

'If this is your idea of a joke, Pardee, consider that I've laughed. Ha ha! Now, pay me! Thirty-five dollars was the agreement at Comanche Junction, and thirty-five dollars is what I want!'

'Joke be damned!' flared Pardee. 'Where money is concerned I never joke.'

Again he would have turned away and again Tracy whirled him back, this time violently. Tracy's gray eyes had turned smoky-dark.

'Thirty-five dollars, Pardee! And while we're at it, fifty more for the granger, John Vail. Seeing you don't intend to deliver it to him, I will. So—come across!'

Ben Pardee jerked his arm free, squared himself.

'Come across, eh? Sure, Tracy. Sure—like this!'

He swung a savage fist.

Had the punch caught Tracy solidly on the jaw, as Pardee intended, it might well have settled things then and there, for there was plenty behind the blow. But the manner in which Pardee had settled himself on spread feet signaled his intention and enabled Tracy to duck away somewhat and to pull his chin down behind the partial protection of a hunched shoulder. That hunched shoulder took up much of the

25

power of the blow, but Pardee's fist skidded on across Tracy's face, cutting his mouth and staggering him.

Ben Pardee was a good thirty burly pounds heavier than Lee Tracy. But Tracy stood fully as tall, even a little more so, and, though wolf-lean about the flanks, carried that deceptive power in the depth of his chest and width of his shoulders. Also, he was faster on his feet than Pardee. So, when Pardee, confident and truculent, charged in to follow up an advantage more fancied than real, Tracy side-stepped and dug a slashing fist into the side of Pardee's blocky face.

Now it was Pardee who was staggered, and as he recovered and came around again, his expression held clear surprise. Also a wary uncertainty, as though he now had something on his hands he wished he hadn't started. Jack Dhu, watching carefully, exclaimed sharply.

'Yellow, by God, I do believe! Get him, kid!'

Tracy needed no urging. Several days of a steadily deepening dislike, plus natural reaction to a sneak punch added to the surge of cold, gusty anger at a deliberate move to beat him out of hard-earned wages. These things turned the fires loose in Tracy. So now he went after his man.

Pardee, backing up a couple of steps, found his shoulders against one of the porch

26

posts, and he reacted like something trapped and cornered. He showed his teeth in a taut pull of desperation and lunged ahead, both fists knotted and swinging.

Blessed with that superior speed, Tracy weaved inside and stopped the charge with a short, twisting, chopping blow to Pardee's mouth that brought a gout of crimson. But before he could move out again, pawing, reaching arms settled about him, hauling tight across his kidneys and the small of his back.

Here Ben Pardee's slow, but burly strength offered an advantage and he set out to make the most of it. He set down with all he had on that bear hug, at the same time lowering his head and driving it forward into Tracy's face. The impact awakened a quick and stunning pain and for a moment Tracy's senses blurred. But these quickly cleared under the bite of a deeper pain as he felt his ribs spring and his spine begin to arch backward.

He fought the pain as he fought his man, swinging from side to side, lunging and whirling, driving Pardee crashing into the store front. Twice he did this, but neither time did it shake the fellow loose or break his grip.

Tracy's heart was thundering, his breath beginning to turn shallow under that locked stricture. Bleak desperation rushed through him. His hands were bunched against Pardee's thick torso, trying to push him clear. Now, with sudden change, he slid the right one upward and drove the heel of it hard against Pardee's blocky chin.

Pardee twisted, trying to avoid this sudden, neck-straining pressure. But Tracy stayed with him, and with another upward surge, snapped Pardee's head far back. For a wrenching moment they held this way. Then Pardee gave a muffled, strangled gasp, his bear hug grip loosened and fell away. And Tracy, lifting on his toes, drove a bunched knee into Pardee's body.

Which brought Pardee over and squarely into a short, savage upper-cut. Pardee's jaw came into view, wobbling. Tracy flailed it, left and right. The first of these punches started Pardee down and the second finished the job, driving him backward off the store porch in a sprawling fall, to roll there in the street's trampled dust.

Still held with the fever of the thing, Tracy started to follow, then caught himself, scrubbing a shirt sleeve across his battered mouth while sucking in great gulps of precious air. He stared down at Ben Pardee, then turned, to find not only Jack Dhu watching him, but also Asa Bingham and a couple of long-faced wagon men.

'Be damned!' Asa Bingham exclaimed. 'So it is you, Lee Tracy! And by the sound of things, like to knock in the front of my store. There's a reason for this?'

Drawing another deep breath, Tracy nodded. 'The best, Asa.' The words came a trifle thickly from a throat harshened by extreme effort. 'That fellow down there tried to do me out of some wages. When I objected, he took a swing at me. So—' A shrug finished this statement, after which Tracy looked at Jack Dhu. 'Just so nobody can argue the point, Jack, maybe you better collect those wages for me.'

'Right!' agreed Jack Dhu. 'Your wages and that granger's damages.'

He dropped down to the street and bent over Ben Pardee, who was so nearly out he made no slightest resistance as the wad of currency was taken from his pocket and eighty-five dollars counted out. Returning the balance, Jack Dhu grinned wickedly and climbed back to the porch.

'He sure made a mistake when he tried to run that blazer. He'll damn well realize that when he gets through gaggin' for air. Kid, you surprise me. I never figured you quite that tough. You sure took him apart!'

One of the wagon men spoke up in a resenting, carping tone.

'Don't know as I like this. Strikes me as a pretty high-handed business, knockin' a man down, then helpin' yourself to his money. No, sir—I don't like it. How do we know you

29

ain't—?'

He broke off so suddenly he strangled slightly. For Jack Dhu had whirled on him with a look which set the fellow back a stride.

'Would you be callin' anybody a liar or a thief?' rapped the fiery Texan. 'You got your foot in your mouth and you're close to chokin' to death on it. Mind your damned business!'

Asa Bingham spoke quickly to head matters off. 'I know Lee Tracy. I know him well. If he says a thing is so, then it is so.'

Tracy pocketed the money Jack Dhu handed him, then added gruffly.

'Thanks, Asa.'

The store owner studied him for a moment, appeared about to say more, then decided against it, turning back inside with a face shadowed and troubled. The two wagon men sidled away, their glances resentful and antagonistic, but their mouths carefully shut.

Jack Dhu stared after them.

'Damn a sniveling, self-righteous man! Always so ready to stick a long nose into some one else's business—'

'One of the poorer parts of human nature, Jack,' said Tracy. 'Now let's get out of here before somebody else comes along to ask fool questions.'

'Get out—where?'

'I know a ranch where we can hole up while we figure future plans.'

30

Jack Dhu shook his head.

'I got no future plans. Gave up having any a long time ago. Trying to figure the future makes life too complicated. Besides, crossing that damn desert left me with a long thirst. I'll be seeing you around.'

Tracy did not argue the point. He'd come to like this lank, cold-jawed Texan. But he recognized a streak of wildness in the man and an almost fanatic sense of personal independence. So now he nodded.

'Fair enough. Good luck until then, Jack.'

His horse was tied at the far end of the store hitch rail. In the saddle, he threaded a way through the crush of wagons crowding the street. A warm moistness seeped down his chin and a hand rubbed across the spot came away stained with crimson. He dabbed at his cut lips with the tail of a badly faded neckerchief, a gust of renewed anger twisting through him. That sure had been a raw one which Pardee tried to pull!

Nearing the edge of town, the tangle on the street forced a halt while a big freight outfit, lead wagon and back action, creaked ponderously by. Just behind the freighter came an open-topped buggy, all bright and new and sparkling in the sun. A matched pair of spirited bay horses drew the rig, and handling the reins with deft control was the person Lee Tracy had been trying for two years to forget.

She saw him the moment he saw her and she set back on the reins and drew her fretting team to a halt. Her dark eyes widened and her full lips parted breathlessly.

'Lee! Lee Tracy!'

He touched his hat.

'Hello, Lucy. Or maybe, all things considered, that's too familiar. I better change it. Mrs Scott, how are you?'

He made no attempt to keep a bitter irony from the words. She was, he decided, just as beautiful as she had been back in the days when she had blinded his eyes and heart so completely—back when she had been Lucy Garland and he'd built some great dreams around her. Her dark eyes, her raven hair, her willful, crimson mouth...

He had flinched slightly.

'I'll forgive you that, Lee, for perhaps I deserve it. But now—oh, it's so good to see you again! And I must talk with you!'

Studying her soberly, Tracy shook his head.

'Afraid your husband would object, Mrs Scott. Our talking was done a long time ago. We did a lot of it then, concerning the two of us. And you never meant a word of it. So I see no profit in any of it now, no profit at all!'

He touched his hat and rode on.

*   *   *

Tasker Scott's office took up one corner of a big, newly built warehouse. He was pacing this, up and down, chewing on an unlighted cigar, when the door swung and his wife entered. He turned on her with some show of impatience.

'What the devil are you doing in town?'

She observed him for a cool moment before making tart reply.

'I felt like driving in, so I did. That was the bargain, remember? You do as you please, I do as I please.' She studied him again before adding, 'I see you know about it.'

'Know about what?'

'That Lee Tracy is back.'

Tasker Scott's lips flattened. 'You've seen him—talked to him?'

She shrugged shapely shoulders. 'I saw him. I'd liked to have talked with him, but he wasn't interested. Not that I blame him. For I really did treat him foul.'

Scott cut a hand sharply through the air in front of him.

'You stay away from him. You don't know him any more.'

Again Lucy Scott looked her husband up and down.

'Would you be jealous, Tasker? You are, of course. You always have been. Jealous of all your possessions. Greedy, too.'

His short, barking laugh was mirthless. 'You're a fine one to talk about greed!'

'Yes,' she admitted frankly, 'I am. You're quite right, there. We are very greedy people, both of us. Two of a kind. A fact I was fully aware of when I married you. For that matter, it was the principal reason I did marry you. In you I thought I saw a man who could get me all the material things I wanted in life.'

It was his turn to survey her critically. What he saw deepened the florid flush in his cheeks, stirred up strange lights in his eyes. His question was clipped.

'Just the material things?'

Now it was she who laughed, and without mirth.

'Of course. You never knew a truly tender emotion in your life. So let's not pretend now. Let's not make any attempt at being sentimental. I'm afraid it would turn into a very poor and unconvincing act. Nauseating, too. Instead, suppose we come down to cases. What are you—we—going to do about him?'

'Tracy, you mean?'

'Exactly. He's back. What about him?'

Tasker Scott dropped into the chair behind his desk. He tried to light his cigar, found it too badly chewed and frayed to draw. So he threw it aside, carefully pared the tip from a fresh one and lit up. He scowled into the smoke for a moment before answering.

'I'll take care of him. I ran him out of Maacama Basin once before. I'll do it again.'

Her retort was quick. 'That's empty talk and you know it. You ran nobody out of Maacama Basin. Lee Tracy left here because he was emotionally hurt and disillusioned, cruelly so. But he has had time to get over it. So now he's back and sure to look up Buck Theodore. He'll hear about the condition of Flat T affairs. Something tells me he won't take that lying down. He could cause us plenty of trouble.'

Tasker Scott blew out a mouthful of smoke, shook his head.

'There's nothing he can do about it. He can't prove a thing.'

Lucy Scott shrugged. 'You've traveled pretty fast, Tasker. Maybe too fast to cover all your trail.'

He pounded the desk with a suddenly angry fist.

'I don't like that kind of talk. It makes me out a crook!'

Lucy laughed again.

'Well, aren't you? Or would you try to persuade a doubting world and your observant wife that you're a thoroughly honest man?'

Tasker Scott turned very quiet, studying her with narrowed glance.

'You are,' he said presently, 'the most beautiful woman I ever saw. And the most cold-blooded. There have been others like you in history, but every now and then a man came forth who knew just how to handle them. I think it is high time you were handled, too!'

He was swiftly out of his chair and had her hard by the arm. His fingers dug deep and she twisted angrily at the pain of it, trying to pull loose.

'Let go of me!'

Instead he hauled her close and kissed her heavily. Then he held her away, jeering.

'My so-loving wife!'

She pulled back her free hand and slapped him across the face.

Instantly he was shaking her until her head began to snap loosely and her hair fell in a shining, ink-black wave across her shoulders. What burned in his eyes was far worse than the physical punishment. So when he let her go she leaned weakly against a wall. For the first time, Lucy Scott was actually afraid of her husband. He saw that fear in her eyes, and laughed.

'Now we really understand each other. I should have brought this understanding about earlier. One final word to you, my dear. You stay away from Lee Tracy!'

She did not answer. With unsteady fingers she tidied up her hair somewhat and smoothed her disordered dress. Wordlessly she went out, passing Ben Pardee just beyond the door. He stared at her stupidly. His eyes were dull and bleary, his lips puffed, and one side of his jaw lumpy with bruise. Both his breathing and his step were unsteady as he went on into the office.

Tasker Scott's greeting was hardly one of welcome.

'Now what in hell do you want?' Scott peered more closely. 'What happened to you? What did you run into?'

'Tracy!' blurted Pardee thickly. 'Lee Tracy. God damn him! Where'll I find the law in this town?'

'Law? There isn't any, yet. What do you want with law?'

Pardee told him, between mumbled curses.

'He went off with eighty-five dollars of my money, Tracy did. I was down and couldn't do anything to stop it. That money was taken right out of my pocket. It was robbery, bare-faced. And I want something done about it!'

Tasker Scott considered him narrowly.

'Pull up a chair. I think we can do business. Right now, as I said, there's no law in Antelope. But maybe I could set up some. How would you like to be town marshal?'

Ben Pardee stared.'Me! Town marshal?'

'Why not? You're a man grown, aren't you? You know how to use a gun. And Tracy is certain to show in town again. When he

37

does it would be a lot of satisfaction to slap an arrest on him yourself, wouldn't it? Besides,' Scott added smoothly, 'you could always hope he'd try and resist arrest. In which case—well, more than one man has stopped a slug because he tried to resist arrest.'

Their glances met and held. Then both nodded. And smiled; though Ben Pardee's effort in this direction was more ugly grimace than anything else. Still and all, they understood each other.

'You got a badge?' Pardee asked.

'I got a badge,' Scott nodded, producing one from a desk drawer.

CHAPTER THREE

Lee Tracy rode north from Antelope along the river trail. What with the combined effects of the long, long hours of last night, and the draining after-effects of his affair with Ben Pardee, he might easily have slept in his saddle, but for the disarray of his thoughts.

Not thoughts of last night's wild, dangerous moments, nor yet of the brawl with Pardee. These were already parts of the past and relegated to their proper places. But thoughts of Lucy Scott.

Lucy Garland Scott...

She too he had believed safely a part of the past. Over the long months of absence from Maacama Basin, image of her had gradually dimmed, until, at the moment of his abrupt decision to return, it seemed she no longer counted at all; that he was completely free of her and of any hold she might have had on him.

Now he wasn't so sure. For it was useless to try and deny the upsurge of feeling he'd known at sight of her, back there in town. True, he'd done a good job of hiding all sign of the feeling behind a mask of curt remoteness, but he couldn't deny the fact of it. At least, not to himself.

He stirred tiredly, pushed a carefully exploring hand across his bruised face and put his attention more closely on the somewhat changed world he rode through. Particularly along these river flats, where, in the lengthening miles from town he had passed a number of granger camps. Some plainly set up but a short time previous, others which had been there for a longer time. Several had already broken ground and put up a flimsy shelter or two.

He wondered about this, for there had been nothing of the sort in the basin when he'd left two years ago. He wondered also what Hack Garland must think of it—arrogant, pompous old Hack, who had

39

for years blustered and bullied his way up and down the basin, throwing his weight at all the smaller ranchers and at anyone else who would stand for it. Never, Tracy recalled, had he ever heard Hack Garland refer to any granger or would-be settler in terms other than a profane and never-changing hatred. Now it seemed there was at least one camp of such in every river meadow.

He left the river trail at Border Creek, crossing this and swinging east along its north bank into rolling, gradually up-climbing grass lands, summer-tawny on the higher slopes, shading into the faintest suggestion of green in the hollows where some trace of surface moisture still held despite the drain of the sun. Open range country which ran on and on to finally blend into the distance-misted, timber-darkened escarpment of Chancellor Peak.

Cattle country, this, and he began passing cattle, here and there, some close at hand, some distant. As he rode he read brands. Presently he was frowning and wondering, and as the miles drifted behind and Chancellor Peak began to loom ever closer, wonderment became nagging uneasiness.

He topped a rounded crest, and with old Chancellor rearing close and abrupt, massive in its timbered bulk, Tracy reined in to have his good look at these well-remembered heights. There was a narrow fault in the flank of the escarpment which was the mouth of Border Canyon, and just off the north point of this, on a low shelf of the slope which gave it some prominence, was the frugal cluster of ranch buildings that marked Flat T headquarters, the layout still held in minutia by distance.

He went on, dropping from the crest to swing through a long hollow where grazed another jag of cattle, and as these drifted aside to let him pass he again read brands and the uneasiness in him deepened. For this north side of Border Creek was Flat T range, and the south side was Lazy Dollar, and while he had read the Lazy Dollar a considerable number of times, he had yet to see a single Flat T.

This was far out of balance. There had always been crossover by cattle of both outfits, some Flat T feeding south of the creek, some Lazy Dollar drifting north of it. But in either case the brands would be mixed, with plenty of both in evidence. Not now, however. Today, even on this north side, nothing showed but Lazy Dollar.

Clearing the long sweep of this final hollow, Tracy had another good survey of headquarters, and he didn't like the look of things. For while the place for the most part stood familiar in his eyes, yet it was different. It was something he felt as well as saw, a

41

feeling that the place was whipped and desolate, while seeing it as run down and neglected. Which wasn't Buck Theodore's way.

Uneasiness became alarm. Buck Theodore—had anything happened to him? To a young man, two years might not loom as of too great account. But at Buck's age...

Tracy sent his horse ahead, climbing the short slope to the place. The corrals were forlornly empty except for a pair of horses. A thin spill of smoke seeped from the ranchhouse chimney. As Tracy hauled up before the door a man stepped through. A stringy man, with a narrow face, a ragged mustache, and hard, suspicious eyes. Across the crook of one arm lay a Winchester carbine. He considered Tracy with a slow deliberateness, then spat and spoke with a nasal drawl.

'You lookin' for somebody?'

Tracy nodded. 'For Buck Theodore.'

The man spat again. 'Never heard of him.'

Alarm quickened in Tracy. Also caution. Something was wrong here, very wrong. He kept his tone and words casual.

'Two years ago a man named Theodore lived here. I've been away. Just thought I'd drop by and say hello.'

He with the carbine called over his shoulder. 'Hey Stump! Come out here!'

The man who now filled the ranchhouse

door was startlingly short and broad, with a roach of coarse, rusty hair above a round pock-marked face.

'Stump,' said the owner of the carbine, 'you ever hear of anybody named Buck Theodore?'

Stump considered, blinking at Tracy.

'Now I don't know,' he said finally. 'What's he look like? How old is he?'

'He's getting on,' Tracy said carefully.

Stump had been eating. Now he belched expansively and waved a casual hand.

'There's a feller hangs out in a line camp cabin north of here by an old timber burn. Might be him, do you think, Bob?'

He of the carbine shrugged. 'Wouldn't know, but could be.' He put his hard survey on Tracy again. 'That's the best we can do for you.'

'I know the place,' Tracy said. 'I'll ride by for a look. Obliged.'

He reined away, burdened with tension and the clutter of dismal thoughts. Why wasn't Buck Theodore at the old headquarters? What had happened during these past two years? What great harm had he done Buck by running off to nurse his own selfish feelings? And how would Buck react on seeing him again? With disgust and contempt? If so, rightly so.

Providing, of course, that those two hard cases back there hadn't lied to him.

43

Providing somebody really was at the old line camp and that the somebody was Buck...

He put several miles behind him before the cloud of doubt thinned enough to let him again take note of his immediate surroundings. When he did, it was to mark the fact that the shadow thrown by his horse and himself had taken on both length and slant. Afternoon was moving along and westward. Far across the basin, the first flow of purple shadow was staining the deeper folds of the Mingo Hills.

The timber burn mentioned by the fellow Stump was better than ten years old, scarring a blunt-nosed ridge that humped outward from the Chancellor Peak escarpment. The line cabin stood just beyond this, and anyone riding north, on rounding past the ridge point, came upon it suddenly.

The cabin was weathered, low-crouched and inconspicuous. A pole corral and three-sided feed shed stood with it. A little ditch, threading the edge of the burn, carried a steady flow of clear water past the place, touching one corner of the corral before running on to lose itself in a small, tule-grown swamp a couple of hundred yards out in the flat.

Nature, with her infinite purpose and patience, had been working on the burn, and while the ridge still bristled with the scattered black and gray bones of fire-killed timber, second growth of several kinds was thrusting vigorously up, eager to hide the desolation of the past.

Tracy's first glance, reaching for proof of the cabin's occupancy, found it in the presence of the lone horse drowsing on three legs in a corner of the corral. The animal, at the soft thump of approaching hoofs, lifted its head, prick-eared and whickered softly.

Tracy, almost fearfully, sent his call.

'Hello—the cabin!'

The half-opened door of the place became fully so and a gaunt, stoop-shouldered man with a seamed, weary face stepped into view. It was Buck Theodore, all right, but a far different looking one than the man Tracy remembered. Here was hair almost snow white, where before there had been only a shading of vigorous grizzle. Here was change, great change. Tracy's throat tightened and when he spoke his words fell huskily.

'Hello, Buck!'

The white-haired old fellow straightened, staring and staring again, as though unable to fully credit what he heard and now saw. He came slowly forward, peering with dimmed eyes.

'Lee, Lee Tracy! Boy! Be damned—oh, be damned—!' The tone was deep and hollow.

Tracy slid from his saddle and they struck hands, old Buck gripping tightly with both of his. Tracy laughed shakily.

'It's great to see you again, Buck, great!'

Answer came slowly in that same deep, hollow tone.

'You ain't seein' much. Just a busted flush that'll never rate another deal. Boy, where you been—where you been?'

There was a plaintive cry in the words.

'Just drifting,' Tracy told him guiltily. 'Have I been away too long?'

'Too long—what is too long? Just so you're back—so you're really back.' The old fellow made an effort to straighten his shoulders. 'Yeah,' he said again, 'jest so you're back. About you bein' gone—I dunno as it would have made much difference had you stayed along—not where the ranch was concerned. Likely enough, Tasker Scott would have been too strong for both of us. Anyway, it's gone, boy, the ranch is gone. Tasker Scott's got it. He took it away from me. I let you down boy, I let you down!'

'No!' Tracy differed, half harshly. 'No, you didn't let me down. It's just the other way around. You didn't run out on me. I ran out on you. Ran like a whipped pup!'

Old Buck dropped a hand on Tracy's shoulder.

'Ain't blamin' you, boy, ain't blamin' you a bit. In your shoes I'd have done the same—mebbe worse. No, not your fault. I know all the fine plans you'd made, all the

46

things you figgered on. You used to talk them over with me, remember? Then Lucy Garland left you flat and married Tasker Scott. A deal like that was enough to toss any man. And while it's probably no great comfort to you, it's common knowledge that by this time Lucy realizes she made a damn poor choice.'

'I wonder,' Tracy said, the old bitterness creeping into his tone. 'Not that she knows—but that she cares?'

'Now there I couldn't say,' Buck admitted. 'For some women's minds can run powerful strange. One thing I do know—Hack Garland sure got what he asked for. He died last spring. I hear he died of shame, because his prize son-in-law finagled him plumb out of his shirt. But shuck that saddle, boy—and corral your bronc,' Buck added, his voice taking on renewed vigor. 'I was just fixin' to throw some supper grub together. Damn! It sure is good to have you here again. Makes me feel like it might be worth while to go on livin' for a time!'

Buck turned back into the cabin, blowing his nose loudly. In the gravest frame of mind he'd ever known, Lee Tracy unsaddled and corraled his horse. A blinding sense of guilt held him. The ranch gone. Faithful old Buck reduced to living a pack-rat existence in a forlorn, tumbledown line cabin. And all because he, Lee Tracy, had let a sultry, black-haired, handsome, but heartlessly self-seeking girl make a craven fool of him.

In the cabin, Buck Theodore had a fire going and was banging pots and pans around. Despite its age and former lack of use, this small, log cubby was now clean and neat. Tracy dropped his war-bag in a corner and moved up beside the stove. 'About the ranch, Buck—what happened?'

While gathering his thoughts for answer, Buck stoked the fire again.

'Like I said, it was Tasker Scott. Slick feller, that hombre is, boy, slick as grease. And crooked—oh, my! He kept hirin' riders away from me. No matter what I'd pay a saddle hand, he'd pay them more. So I had to do the best I could holdin' things together by myself. I tried, all right. I worked twenty hours a day. But I couldn't be everywhere at once. I'd miss a jag of cattle here, and while I was tryin' to trail 'em down, another bunch would disappear somewhere else.' Buck paused, his gaunt face pulling into brooding soberness. Then he shrugged. 'A year and a half of that kind of going over and I was all done.'

'That's about the cattle. But the ranch?' Tracy prompted.

Buck shrugged again.

'Had to borrow money to keep goin' as long as I did. Asa Bingham let me have three thousand on a mortgage note, with the

48

spread as collateral. Six months later, Scott showed up with the note, demanding payment. He'd bought the note from Bingham. I couldn't rake up enough right then to think of payin' off, which Scott well knew. Oh, I might have stalled him off for a while, but the way things were going I wouldn't have had the money then, either. And I was tired of fightin' something I couldn't stop. A man gets old, boy—then the will to fight kinda leaks out of him. So I jest hauled out from under the whole damn mess—and the hell with it! That was how I felt. Mebbe had I been ten years younger I might have throwed a gun on Tasker Scott and shot his greedy heart out.'

Outwardly, Lee Tracy was still. Inwardly he was writhing under the unconsciously accusing weight of old Buck's words. Had he stayed on and lent his energy to the cause, then all this might never have happened. As it was...

Tracy cleared his throat. 'The cattle that Scott rustled, Buck. Where did they end up?'

A third time Buck twitched a shoulder.

'God knows—I don't. I've prowled this basin from end to end and read brands until I'm damn near blind—and I ain't seen a single beef critter in the past six months packin' our old Flat T brand. I dunno where Scott took 'em, but he sure did a job of it. And any few he might have missed have likely enough ended up in some granger's pot by this time. Anyway, it's all water under the bridge, now.'

'Maybe,' Tracy said tersely. 'Maybe.'

'No maybe,' declared Buck. 'It just is. You come in from Antelope?'

'Yes. I came through town.'

'Then you saw how things is changed. Boy, we got damn near an all-out land rush on here in Maacama Basin. There's talk that Tasker Scott engineered it, so's he could clean up on the property he's got hold of. Which he owns plenty, in Antelope and round about. I understand he's even gamblin' on makin' a big killin' in property when the railroad brings a branch line into the basin.'

'Railroad!' Tracy was startled. 'Here—in Maacama Basin? That will never happen.'

Buck scooped flour into a pan and began mixing biscuit dough.

'Long time ago I quit tellin' myself that this or that would never happen. I got fooled too many times. Now there jest about ain't nothin' I'd flat out say wouldn't ever happen. Because the world keeps movin' along. Mebbe we don't exactly like the direction, but we got to go along. Because there ain't a smidgin of a chance to hold it back. Not for long, anyhow.

'Hell, boy! I can remember this country when there was jest me and Hack Garland

and Spence Mulholland and Manuel Rojas runnin' cattle in it. Antelope wasn't even a wide place in the trail. We brought our livin' supplies in by pack horse plumb across the desert from Comanche Junction. And with Manuel Rojas straddlin' the river gap, who'd ever believed we'd someday see grangers inside this basin? Why the river flats are crawlin' with 'em. No, boy—don't ever say this or that can't happen. For sure as shootin', you'll come up wrong.'

'All right,' Tracy conceded. 'We'll say the railroad might come in. What's Scott's big deal there?'

'Simple,' Buck explained. 'There's only two ways a railroad could come in. Either by the river gap, or by Smoky Pass. And who's got the country sewed up in both places? Why Mister Tasker Scott, of course. Hankerin' to see Mexico again before he died, Manuel Rojas sold out his river gap holdings to Scott. And Scott owns most of the land this side of Smoky Pass, where the railroad would have to cut through. I'm tellin' you, boy, that feller don't miss a trick.'

For a little time, Tracy was silent, held with frowning speculation. Then his head came up.

'How did Scott get hold of the land around Smoky Pass, Buck?'

'Bought it up, I guess.'

'He couldn't do that,' Tracy said. 'That

51

was government land, open to homestead, but not for sale.'

Buck considered a moment, then gave another of his fatalistic shrugs.

'I dunno exactly how he got it, but he's got it. I was lookin' at a land office map a while back and jest about all the slope this side the pass was blocked in solid—under Tasker Scott's name.'

'But he couldn't have bought it,' argued Tracy. 'He couldn't get hold of that land without going through all the rules and regulations of homesteading, improvements and occupancy—all that sort of thing. Buck, somethin's crooked there.'

'With Scott mixed in, I'd expect it to be,' declared Buck. 'But here's what you're overlookin', boy. In Maacama Basin, Tasker Scott does jest about as he damn well pleases. When he cracks the whip, even them in the land office dance. You'd think, bein' government men, they wouldn't have to. Yet they do. Yes, sir, Mister Tasker Scott may be crooked as a broken-backed snake, but he's the slickest article ever to hit these parts.'

Lee Tracy got out his smoking, spun up a cigarette. He paced the short area of the cabin, again held in frowning speculation. He paused presently.

'You know, Buck, there is one big mistake every crook always makes.'

'So—o?' Buck put a pan of biscuits in the

52

oven, straightened and came around. 'How's that?'

'They go drunk on their own smartness. That's what makes them a crook in the first place, figuring they can outsmart everybody else. They figure the world is full of suckers, ready for them to fleece. Actually, they're the truly stupid ones, for figuring they can beat the game. So, before they get through, they end up outsmarting themselves.'

'That sounds all right,' concurred Buck cautiously, still held with an old man's tired pessimism. 'But some of them fellers take a lot of catchin' up with. Boy, I know how you feel. You've come back to something that's pretty tough to swallow. Still and all, the best thing you can do is jest swallow and let it go at that. Because you can't ride against this feller, Scott. He's got the money, the power, and the guns behind him.'

A sack, hanging from a rafter, held a haunch of venison. From this, Buck sliced off some generous steaks, doused them in flour, then slid them into a skillet that had begun to sizzle and snap with hot bacon grease. Then the old fellow went on.

'Don't you go gettin' any foolish ideas about owin' me anything, because you don't. I can sleep warm and dry right here in this cabin and long as there's deer in the gulches I won't go hungry. And like I said, I don't give much of a damn any more, any how.

But you—you're still young and got lots of time ahead of you. You can make a new start somewhere else. There jest ain't no sense in your runnin' a chance of gettin' killed around here for nothin'.'

Tracy studied the old fellow through the cabin gloom, then nodded slowly.

'Sure, Buck, sure,' he said gently. 'Of course you'd say something like that. Trying to make it easy for me. But not for yourself. Don't tell me you wouldn't like to sit again on the porch of the old ranchhouse and look down across the flats at cattle, your own cattle, feeding there on Flat T range. Old or young, Buck, don't tell me you wouldn't like that. I know better.'

Buck turned away quickly, his voice running high and tight.

'Boy, you're puttin' colors in the sky that jest ain't there. The old spread belongs to Tasker Scott, now—and he's got a couple of his own pet breed of saddle hands holding it down for him. Tough ones, I mean.'

'I saw them,' Tracy nodded. 'Where did they come from?'

'Wouldn't know. Somewhere outside. When Tasker Scott started to grab at this and that, he brought in them and some others like 'em. Rough customers, boy. And neither me or the old layout is worth you tanglin' with that crowd.'

'I think you are,' said Tracy quietly. 'I

might have run once, Buck. But no more. I've got my full growth now. And over the past couple of years I've learned considerable. One more question. Did you ever give Tasker Scott a bill of sale for anything?'

Buck came around, staring. 'Hell, no! I wouldn't sell that feller dirt for gold. What's that got to do with it?'

Tracy showed a quick grin. 'You might be surprised. So might Mister Scott. We'll see.'

CHAPTER FOUR

Lee Tracy was early in the saddle. He had eaten heartily, slept soundly, then eaten heartily again, and so was thoroughly renewed, both physically and in spirit. For though he had found Buck Theodore in circumstances far from what he had expected, at least he had found him, alive and well. From the old fellow he had had full picture of the events and conditions responsible for this state of affairs, and now he was abroad this day to do something about it.

He was riding well ahead of the sun, with night's vitality and freshness still rising from the earth to sweeten the air in a man's nostrils and put vigor in his veins. Over west, the Mingos loomed dark and still, but in the east, beyond the Chancellor Peak escarpment, the sky had begun to pale slightly and show the first faint hint of sunrise color. And though that moment was still near a half hour away, a water-clear light lay suddenly across the land, and objects that had been dim and shadowy stood out sharp and distinct.

Rather than swing west to the river trail and thus cover the longer route, he crossed Border Creek a full mile below Flat T headquarters and rode the reaching angle straight for town. The sun caught up with him well short of here and by the time he rode into Antelope, full hint of the day's heat to come, hung in the air.

Town was no less active than it had been yesterday afternoon and he had to seek the far end of the hitch rail in front of Asa Bingham's store to find a place for his horse. He dismounted and tied and headed for the land office. Where a saloon front ran, he paused beside a lank figure hunkered down in brooding stillness.

'Get rid of that thirst, Jack?'

Jack Dhu's head came slowly up, showing a pair of bloodshot eyes and a crooked grin.

'Swapped it for a hell of a headache.'

'Reckless man,' Tracy murmured. 'Had breakfast?'

Jack Dhu considered for a moment, while

56

feeling cautiously in his pockets. Presently he shrugged. 'Ain't hungry.'

'Now there's a proud and cheerful liar,' observed Tracy to the world at large. 'Come along. And don't go stiff-necked on me.'

Jack Dhu pushed carefully to his feet, blinking painfully.

'Have a good look at a damn fool. I'm taking you up because right now I need black coffee like a drowning man needs air.'

They turned into an eating house and found places at the counter.

'I've had my breakfast,' Tracy said. 'But you dig in. Afterwards, I got a proposition to offer.'

When they returned to the street some half hour later, Jack Dhu built a cigarette and had his look at the world out of less jaundiced eyes.

'Me, I'm beginning to live again,' he admitted, almost cheerfully. 'And short of walkin' on my hands, which I never could do, I'll trail along at whatever you got in mind.'

'First,' said Tracy, 'let's try the land office.'

In here the clerk was sharp-featured and plainly fancied himself as somewhat of a dandy. Also as a personage of considerable importance, with the right and intention to put all lesser folk in their places. With the half-dozen grangers who were in line ahead of Tracy he was markedly brusque and curt.

When his turn came, Tracy called for a map of the west side of the basin, which he frowned over for a moment.

'These blocked in sections show land already taken?'

'That's it.' The clerk's manner was very officious.

'And the map is up to date?'

'Of course.'

Tracy indicated a certain area. 'Who homesteaded this part?'

'Does it matter? The map plainly shows the land is taken.'

Tracy fixed the clerk with a chill survey.

'Friend, I asked you a straight question. I want a straight answer. Who homesteaded this area?'

'Yeah,' seconded Jack Dhu. 'A straight answer. We ain't some half-whipped granger to be buffaloed around by such as you. So you talk up, and talk straight!'

The clerk's haughty manner became a harried one. These two riders facing him through the wicket were suddenly forbidding.

'I'll check,' he said hastily. 'Take a couple of minutes.'

He went to some files which he appeared to study carefully before announcing his findings.

'The records show that area as taken up by

58

Mr Scott, Mr Tasker Scott.'

Lee Tracy showed a sardonic grin.

'Knew that all the time, didn't you? Now let's have some more straight answers. Did Mister Tasker Scott actually homestead that land strictly according to every requirement of the law? Did he fulfill all the occupancy and improvement conditions?'

The clerk's harried look now resolved into a confused and flustered one.

'Why I suppose—I guess he did. You'd have to see Mr Wilkens about that. Mr Wilkens is the land agent. I just work here.'

Tracy's sardonic grin widened. 'Oh, sure, sure! And you want to remember that. It could save you trouble in the future.'

As they moved out into the street, Jack Dhu simmered.

'You ever see it fail? Some jigger gets himself a two-bit government job and right away he begins throwin' his weight around, like he was plumb superior to ordinary folks. I sure enjoy stickin' a pin in that sort and watch 'em shrink as the gas leaks out.'

Tracy shrugged. 'Little man in a little job, trying to appear big. Get your horse, Jack—we're taking a ride. I'll wait for you at the store.'

Jack Dhu had put his horse up for the night at the livery corrals, so now he nodded and angled away. Tracy returned to the store where Asa Bingham, sweeping out, was finishing this chore on the porch. He leaned on his broom and fixed Tracy with a sober glance.

'Now you're in these parts, do you aim to stay?' he asked gruffly.

Tracy nodded. 'That's it.'

'You know where Buck Theodore is?'

'I spent the night with him.'

'What do you think of the shape he's in?'

There was an implication here that brought a faint flush to Tracy's face.

'I don't like it,' he said simply.

Bingham, still accusing, said, 'You sure left the old fellow to take a hell of a beating.'

'Yes,' Tracy admitted quietly, 'I did. And you didn't help any when you sold that note to Tasker Scott.'

Bingham bobbed a sober head.

'That's right. Biggest mistake I ever made in my life. I didn't know Scott then like I know him now. He gave me his solemn word he wouldn't press Buck. I was short of the cash at the time, which is why I sold. And I've felt like hell about it ever since.'

There was no mistaking the sincerity of Bingham's words. Tracy slapped him on the shoulder.

'We both made mistakes, Asa. But maybe we can do something about correcting them. Buck and me, we may need a little credit for a time. That's how you can help.'

The storekeeper's glance narrowed

60

shrewdly. 'You got some thing under your hat. What is it?'

'Have one hell of a try at getting the ranch back for Buck.'

Bingham massaged his bony chin with thumb and forefinger.

'Tough chore, Lee. Damn tough chore. Tasker Scott's got a mighty tight grip on this basin, and if I know the feller, he aims to hang on.'

'He'll try,' Tracy agreed.

'It could end in gunsmoke,' warned Bingham. 'Which is never good.'

'Never good,' agreed Tracy again. 'But sometimes necessary.'

Asa Bingham gave him another careful survey. 'Strikes me you've pretty well grown up, Lee.'

Tracy grinned faintly. 'Man's bound to, Asa. How about that credit?'

The storekeeper began wielding his broom again. 'Any time,' he said gruffly.

Tracy turned to look along the street, impatient for Jack Dhu's arrival. And so saw Ben Pardee step to the store porch and come along it, striding heavily. Just as heavily, Pardee threw his purpose ahead of him.

'Tracy—I want you!'

Tracy measured him warily. 'I'd have thought you had plenty of me yesterday. You start it again, Pardee, it could be worse.'

Pardee's swollen lips pulled angrily.

61

'Smart as hell, you are! Well, chew on this. You're under arrest!'

Again Tracy measured him, now noting the badge he wore.

'Arrest! What for? And who says so?'

'I say so! And you know damn well what for. Robbery! I'm taking your gun.'

Tracy did not move. 'I'm not packing a gun. And just for the hell of it, who did I rob, and when?'

'You robbed me,' accused Pardee. 'Yesterday. You and that other damn no-good, that feller Dhu. You went through my pocket and took my money.'

'Not your money, Pardee,' Tracy said. 'Just mine. The wages you owed me and tried to get out of paying. Also, what you owed John Vail for damages. I'm taking that money to him when I leave town a few minutes from now.'

'You're not leaving town,' Pardee declared in his heavy blurting way. 'I'm taking you in—for robbery!'

'No,' said Tracy softly. 'No!'

Ben Pardee slid a hand under his jumper, brought it out full of gun.

'You want to argue?'

The words held more than just the bones of a question. Also they carried an ill-concealed and turgidly ugly eagerness beyond mistaking.

Tracy laughed curtly. 'Won't do, Pardee.

Won't do at all! You get no cheap excuse to shoot me. Asa, who sets up the law in this town?'

'We haven't had any since Joe Spikes quit as marshal a while back,' Bingham said. 'I have a voice in appointing a new man to the job, and I don't know anything about this fellow. I smell another of Tasker Scott's high and mighty moves.' The storekeeper surveyed Ben Pardee with an acid speculation. 'Mister, you take that badge back to Scott before it gets you into big trouble. You got no authority in this town unless I add my sayso. Which I don't!'

'I guess that does it, Pardee,' mocked Tracy.

'No, by God!' stormed Pardee, not to be done out of his advantage. 'I came after you, Tracy—and I'm going to take you!'

He edged in, gun bearing steadily on Tracy's body. There was no mistaking the look in his eyes. On the merest thread of an excuse, Pardee was prepared to shoot. And he was avid for that excuse.

The town's old livery stable and compound lay well back from the street. Leaving here, Jack Dhu rode through the alley at one end of Asa Bingham's store. Emerging from this he looked about for Lee Tracy. His first glance took in Tracy, Ben Pardee, and the gun Pardee held with such open threat. Instantly the Texan drew a gun

63

of his own and his warning came as a high, climbing drone.

'Drop that gun, Pardee—drop it!'

Ben Pardee grunted and his head jerked around. Using the spurs, Jack Dhu surged up just beyond the hitch rail, the weapon he held all cold menace.

For a long moment or two it seemed that Pardee was going to stand fast. Then the shifting lights of indecision flickered in his eyes, his beefy shoulders slumped and he lowered his gun. Which wasn't enough for Jack Dhu, who hit out again in that high and toneless drone.

'Drop it, I said!'

Pardee gave a gusty sigh and his gun clattered on the worn boards of the porch.

'Better,' said Jack Dhu, his voice leveling off. 'What's going on here?'

Tracy explained. The Texan showed a hard grin.

'No! This fellow a marshal? With his color? Why that's an insult to honest men. Take it off, Pardee—the badge, I mean. Take it off!'

Ben Pardee mustered a last thread of argument. 'I was hired to wear this badge. I got authority.'

'Not any!' cut in Dhu coldly. 'Take that badge off and throw it in the street!'

Again indecision touched Pardee, but not for long. In a matter of this sort, once you began to slip, there was no way to stop. He unpinned the badge and threw it in the street.

Jack Dhu showed a searing contempt. 'This is the second blazer you've tried to run. Don't ever try a third. Now get out!'

All resistance had left Pardee. He turned and went away, so possessed with a bottled-up, helpless fury, he weaved from side to side, his stride a heavy shamble.

Jack Dhu, watching him, spat in the dust. 'Yellow all through.'

'Now I wouldn't be too sure of that,' differed Asa Bingham with some severity. 'You couldn't have scarred him worse if you'd horse-whipped him. I've seen his kind before. They take a lot of stirring up, but when they do go on the warpath—look out!'

Jack Dhu shrugged. 'Any time he wants to show some real fire, I'll be glad to have a look.' He put his glance on Tracy. 'Where's your gun?'

'In my war-bag, some distance from here,' Tracy admitted ruefully.

'Damn poor place—considering.'

'I think so,' Tracy said dryly. He picked up Pardee's gun, jacked the cartridges from it, handed the weapon to Bingham. 'He comes looking for it, Asa, give it to him. And obliged, for everything. You'll be seeing me around.'

He went to his horse, lifted to the saddle

and swung in beside Jack Dhu. 'Obliged to you, too, my friend. Pardee had me dead to rights. I didn't have much choice. Let him lock me up, or shoot me—one or the other.'

'A gun,' observed the Texan sententiously, 'ain't worth a damn unless it's where you can lay a hand on it when you need it. From now on, seein' you own one—pack it!'

Asa Bingham watched Tracy and Jack Dhu ride out of town. He frowned down at the gun Tracy had put in his hand, then swung his head and surveyed the street where Ben Pardee's badge had landed. Presently he went out there, waited for a freighter and a spring wagon to pass, then scuffed about in the dust with his toe until he uncovered the badge. This, along with the gun, he carried into his store.

Further up the street, a distinctly agitated land office clerk hurried into Tasker Scott's office where, at the moment, Scott and Rufe Wilkens, the land agent, had their heads together over Scott's desk.

Rufe Wilkens was a swarthy, coarse-featured man, partially bald, with the blue jowls of one whose razor was hard put to keep ahead of a heavy beard. His eyes were small and dark and shrewd. He looked at his clerk with some disapproval.

'You've no business here, Kenna, with the office untended.'

'I thought Mr Scott should know about

66

this right away,' the clerk defended. 'Of course if he doesn't want to—'

He turned as though to leave.

'A minute, Kenna!' rapped Tasker Scott. 'What should I know?'

'About the two riders who were in the office.'

'What two riders?'

'I can't tell you what two. I never saw either of them before.'

'All right—what about them?'

'They asked to see the map of the west side,' explained Kenna. 'They were particularly curious about the area just below Smoky Pass.'

Tasker Scott came forward in his chair, showing a quick glitter of real interest.

'Curious—how?'

'Well, they wanted to know who owned that land.'

'What did you tell them?'

'That you did.'

'You didn't have to tell them that,' said Scott sharply. 'You didn't have to tell them a damn thing.'

Disgruntled at the censure he was taking, Mark Kenna shrugged.

'There were two of them. They were rough and they insisted on knowing. What else could I do but tell them?'

'All right, all right!' Scott exclaimed impatiently. 'So you told them. What happened then? What else did they want?'

'Why,' said Kenna, with just the faintest inflection of satisfaction, 'they wanted to know if you had homesteaded the land and if you had complied with all the requirements of the law as regards the necessary occupancy and development.'

Tasker Scott settled slowly back in his chair, his lips tightening.

'And what was your answer there?'

'I told them they'd have to see Wilkens. That he was the land agent, not me. They left, then.'

'The riders,' Scott asked, 'what did they look like?'

Kenna considered a moment, then gave brief descriptions.

Scott nodded. 'Tracy, of course,' he ground out savagely. 'It would be him!'

Rufe Wilkins showed a pair of raised eyebrows. 'Who the hell is Tracy?'

Tasker Scott hung on his answer slightly. 'A drifter who was around the basin a couple of years ago. He got in my way and I ran him out.'

'But now he's back,' murmured Wilkens. 'And asking questions. Awkward ones. It would seem you didn't run him far enough.'

'I'll take care of him again,' Scott said curtly. He looked at Kenna. 'Anything else?'

'No.' Kenna moved to the door, where, still stung from Scott's attitude, he paused

68

and dropped a final remark. 'Thanks for all my trouble. Next time I'll just answer questions and let it go at that.'

The retort brought the blood to Scott's face and it stayed there as he stared angrily at the empty doorway.

'Would that fellow be getting too large size for his own good?'

Rufe Wilkens shrugged. 'I don't think so. After all, he was trying to do you a favor. It wouldn't have hurt to have said thanks, even if the word he brought was something you didn't like to hear.'

Scott slapped an angry hand on the desk top.

'He didn't have to blab to Tracy the way he did.'

Rufe Wilkens slouched back in his chair, located a cheroot in his vest pocket and, while he lit up, held Tasker Scott with his shrewd, gimlet-eyed glance.

'What are you so damn jittery about? This fellow Tracy, is he nine feet high?'

Scott pushed to his feet, swung about the office a couple of times before answering.

'Hardly. But he could cause us trouble, sticking his nose into our affairs.'

'Perhaps,' conceded Wilkens evenly. 'But not too likely. I'm the land agent in these parts and expect to remain such unless and until Washington says other wise. And that isn't likely. At least not until it won't matter, one way or the other.'

'A word in the wrong place could cause us trouble,' Scott persisted.

'Out here, such a word and the right place for it are a long way apart,' Wilkens observed through a cloud of cheroot smoke. 'And I think I know bureau procedure pretty well. Once they take form, government records are pretty hard to change, if for no better reason than the well known red tape involved. So simmer down, simmer down! If this fellow Tracy gets too much in the way there's always—well—means—!' Wilkens shrugged, meaningly.

Tasker Scott took another turn across the office before settling again into his chair.

'We'll see,' he said shortly. 'Now let's get on with our business.'

Near an hour later, Rufe Wilkens left Tasker's office for the street. His cheroot was smoked down to a stub long since gone cold, and Wilkens had mouthed this until it was just a bitter, soggy remnant. So now he spat it out with distaste and searched his pockets for a fresh smoke. Finding none, he went along a door or two and turned into the Trail House Bar. Here he bought a handful of his favorite brand. While stowing them carefully in a vest pocket, he speculatively eyed a customer further along.

Ben Pardee had both elbows hooked on the bar top and his head and shoulders were hunched over. He had a glass between his hands and a whiskey bottle in front of him. He had already lowered the bottle considerably and even as Wilkens watched, poured himself another heavy jolt and downed it with a quick toss of his head.

After which he seemed to feel the impact of Wilkens's interest, for he made a slow half-wheel and showed a face gone slack and flushed with whiskey.

'Somethin' interestin' you?' he demanded, words slurred and sullen.

The speculation faded from Wilkens's eyes. 'Yes. When I went into Tasker Scott's office a while back, I met you coming out. You were carrying a marshal's badge, then. What happened to it? Understand, I'm merely curious.'

'To hell with you!' mumbled Pardee thickly, turning back to his bottle.

Rufe Wilkens could be a rough man in his own right, so now he rolled up on his toes and for a moment hot fires flared in his eyes. Then he caught himself, turned and went out and crossed to the land office. At the moment the place was empty but for Mark Kenna who was fussing over some records. Wilkens jerked an indicating head toward a rear room.

'Back here, Mark.'

Kenna followed a trifle fearfully. The room was small, with a battered desk and a

71

couple of equally well used chairs. Kenna faced Wilkens across the desk, showing a sulky hesitancy.

'I couldn't help throwing back at Scott. I was only trying to do him a favor.'

'So I told him,' Wilkens said. 'Scott's in such a hurry about everything he tramples people unnecessarily. I'm going to slow him down, even if I have to get tough about it. Now here is what I want you to do. I want you to find out all you can about this fellow Tracy. You heard Scott say that Tracy was around here a couple of years ago, and that he ran him out. Well, I want to know more about that affair. So you circulate and ask questions. I'll take care of the office until you get back.'

From one pocket Mark Kenna took a small rectangle of husk, and from another a pinch of thready, black tobacco, and with these two ingredients built himself a long, thin cigarette. He lit this with equal care and sucked the smoke deep into his lungs.

Watching him, Rufe Wilkens shuddered. 'You don't look it, but you must have the constitution of an ox to smoke that stuff.'

Kenna smiled jauntily and waved the cigarette between deeply stained fingers. 'A man's smoke,' he proclaimed.

'If you think so,' said Wilkens. 'But before it sneaks up on you and strikes you dead, get me the word on Tracy.'

Kenna hesitated. 'If Tasker Scott knows so much about him, you'd think he'd have told you all worth telling.'

'Wouldn't you, now?' agreed Wilkens drily. 'The very fact that he didn't is why I want you to investigate.'

'Fair enough,' Kenna said. 'If there's anything to dredge up, I'll uncover it.'

'Don't beat any drums while you're about it.'

'No drums,' promised Kenna, heading out.

CHAPTER FIVE

It was wash day in the John Vail camp. One line of wash, strung between two trees, was already drying. Beside the river a brisk fire burned, with more water heating over it. Humming to herself as she worked, Kip Vail was bent over a wash-tub, up to her elbows in sudsy foam, scrubbing industriously. And even at this homely chore showing a quick, active grace.

In a warm, shallow backwater of the river the two younger Vail children scurried and splashed, trying with cupped hands to scoop a minnow from the darting swarm about their bare feet. A girl of six with pigtails so tightly braided they stuck straight out from

73

her round little head. A boy of eight, brown-faced and intent. If any remnant of last night's danger and fear remained in this camp, it was nowhere visible.

A click of hoofs on gravel caused Kip Vail to straighten and turn, trying to blow aside a lock of hair that had fallen across her face. She found herself looking up at Lee Tracy. Over at the backwater, Jack Dhu had hauled rein and was smiling down at the two youngsters there, who faced him shyly but sturdily.

Again Kip Vail tried to blow aside the interfering lock of hair, and with little success. Unmindful of the suds on her hands she tried to brush back the stubborn lock and in consequence left a soapy smear across her cheek. Lee Tracy chuckled.

'My mother used to quote a jingle about a little girl who had a little curl, right in the middle of her forehead.'

'And when she was good she was very, very good, and when she was bad she was horrid,' finished Kip Vail. After which they both laughed.

Startled though she had been, this girl was now completely at ease, and Lee Tracy, looking into a pair of clear, blue eyes, thought that she would always be poised and self-reliant, come what would. Though now she colored slightly under the intentness of his glance.

'If I look a fright,' she said, 'it is because it's that kind of a day. For whoever was at their best, up to their eyes in soapsuds?'

'I was thinking you looked particularly well—and useful,' Tracy told her.

Warmer color washed through her cheeks and her eyes dropped. Tracy changed the subject.

'Where's your father?'

John Vail answered this himself by appearing from high up-slope, reining along a harnessed team of solid bay horses that had a length of chain dragging behind them. He left the team at the big wagon, spoke a word or two to his wife who was busy mixing a pan of bread on the tail-board of the wagon, then tramped down to stand beside his daughter, showing no great friendliness as he nodded curtly to Tracy.

'Just finished dragging off that horse of yours that broke its neck falling over my wagon tongue last night,' he said brusquely. 'A chore you could have taken care of yourselves, if you'd wanted to be really fair.'

The girl turned on him. 'Dad, please! This is another day.'

'Maybe,' came the curt retort. 'Just the same, when we woke up this morning, there was that dead horse, right in the middle of our camp.'

John Vail had not missed that flag of warm color in his daughter's cheek, and he did not approve of it, for in him was the grudging, deep-seated distrust owned by all grangers toward saddle men. He shot his blunt question at Tracy.

'Something you wanted?'

'Yes.' Tracy stepped from his saddle and produced some folded greenbacks from a pocket. 'Came by to see you about a couple of things. One was to settle that damage claim of yours. You said fifty dollars would cover it. Here's your money.'

John Vail stared at the money laid in his palm.

'This surprises me,' he admitted gruffly. 'I never expected to collect. Because that feller Pardee wasn't too happy over the idea of paying, besides striking me as being—well, a little on the slippery side.'

'Very much on the slippery side,' Tracy agreed dryly. 'Still and all, he decided to pay.'

'What made him decide?'

Tracy met Vail's glance and smiled faintly. 'This and that.'

'I see,' murmured the granger, marking the lingering stain of a couple of bruises on Tracy's face. 'Yeah, I see,' he went on, his manner mellowing somewhat. 'Obliged, of course. It's a mite unusual to run into a square saddle man.'

'Lots of square ones,' Tracy defended. 'Just a question of meeting up with them.'

76

Again John Vail eyed Tracy carefully. 'You said there were a couple of things you wanted to see me about. What, besides bringing this money?'

Tracy swung an arm, indicating the area round about. 'You homesteading, or just using this for a place to throw down a camp?'

The granger stiffened. 'Homesteading, of course. Anybody questioning my right?'

Tracy shook his head. 'Not me.'

'Would there be somebody else?'

'Maybe. Anyhow, if I were you, I'd make certain my records in the land office were right and complete. After which, I'd hang on to my land, come hell or high water.'

'That,' said John Vail, 'has a damn funny sound. What's behind it?'

'Maybe nothing, maybe a lot. There's some talk going around that the railroad may build a branch line in from Comanche Junction. Should that prove out, it could come in through Smoky Pass. Which should mean something to you.'

'It does, of course!' ejaculated Vail. 'You sure of this?'

Tracy shrugged. 'I'd call it a fair gamble. It'll prove out if somebody tries to argue tough with you over the land.'

'Who'd be liable to do that?' Vail demanded.

'Could be a fellow named Scott—Tasker Scott.'

Vail scoffed.

'That don't make sense. Tasker Scott is the man who opened this basin to folks like me and mine, who encouraged us to come in and settle. Before that, a handful of greedy cattlemen had the basin locked up tight. Even though a lot of it was government land, open for homesteading, they wouldn't let us in. Mr Scott changed all that. No, your talk don't make sense.'

Tracy shrugged again, turned to his horse and swung up. He looked at Kip Vail and touched his hat, and spoke directly to her.

'Another thing my mother used to say. "The devil a saint would be." You remind your father of that, should Tasker Scott or any of his bucko boys come prowling.'

Looking over his shoulder he called, 'All right, Jack!'

He rode away up-river, and Jack Dhu dropped in beside him.

John Vail scowled after them, muttering, repeating to himself, 'Such talk don't make sense.'

'Don't be too sure of it, Father,' offered Kip Vail. 'We're new here, and after all, what do we really know about this Tasker Scott?'

John Vail brought his glance around to his daughter, studying her for a moment.

'I can give that right back to you. What do we really know about this fellow Tracy?'

Kip did not retreat. 'We know that last

night, at the very real risk of his own life, he saved me from being trampled by a band of stampeding horses. And he just put the money in your hand to pay for the damage done. He didn't have to do either of these things. He could have ridden free and safe ahead of those horses, and never bothered about me, and he could have let you whistle for the money.'

John Vail showed a touch of uncertainty. 'You're some taken with that fellow, aren't you?'

Color again flooded Kip's cheeks, but she stood up staunchly to her father's frowning scrutiny.

'I appreciate what he's done for me—for us. I wouldn't be human if I didn't.'

John Vail appraised this slim daughter of his carefully, aware of the fact that she was no longer a child, but a prideful, highly capable young woman in her own right.

'Of course I appreciate those things, too,' he admitted gruffly. 'Only I find it hard to swallow the talk against Tasker Scott. It just doesn't add up.'

Kip dried her hands on her apron, then tucked the vagrant lock of hair securely back of one ear. 'It wouldn't hurt, Father, to check the land office records again.'

John Vail stared away across the basin, considering. 'I'll think on it,' he conceded finally, turning away and going back up slope to the wagon.

For a little time, Kip stood quietly, held by her thoughts. This was a pleasant world round about, just the most pleasant she'd ever seen. And, she mused, she had seen a lot of country since she was old enough to notice such things. For most of her years that big wagon up there yonder had been her home. Oh, along the way there had been a lath and tar paper layout here, or a cabin there. But never for long. Either the land itself was too hostile, with no real future to be wrung from it, or if it was good land, then it was always coveted by somebody with more power than John Vail could cope with. So always it was a case of move on, move on.

The climbing sun, striking past the river growth, was warm and good. Above, the tawny slope of the Mingo Hills climbed in long, wide sweeps. And somewhere up there, where the crest ran into the sky's far, clear space, a hawk sent down its wild, hunting cry. Which a quail, safe in thick covert beside the river, defied with its own plaintive, whistled insolence. In the shallows, momentary capture of a wriggling fragment of finned silver, brought a cry of triumph from the little pigtailed girl.

Smiling, Kip Vail savored every drop of the moment's charm. Then she sighed deeply. Here, at this spot, hopes for permanency had been high. Now it seemed that the old uncertainty, the old doubt was once more at hand.

Again she sighed, then bent to her washing.

★   ★   ★

In the line camp cabin they were eating noon meal, Lee Tracy, Buck Theodore and Jack Dhu. When Tracy had introduced Buck to Jack Dhu, the old fellow had taken his quick, keen survey of the Texan, then welcomed him with a brief but solid hand shake. Now Buck looked across the table at Tracy.

'So you had your look at the land office map of the west side. Satisfied that I knew what I was talking about?'

Tracy nodded. 'You were right. Everything around Smoky Pass is blocked in under Tasker Scott's name.'

'Sure,' said Buck, bobbing his head. 'And that's Tasker for you. He ain't overlookin' nothin' where there's a chance for profit. Mighty shrewd hombre, that feller.'

'Yeah, shrewd,' Tracy said. 'But we'll see if he's been shrewd enough.'

Buck chewed reflectively for a moment, then went on slowly.

'Way I see it, Tasker figgers he's sittin' so tight in the saddle he just don't have to give a damn. Which is likely so. He's sure got some hardcases to back his hand. Like them two he's got holed up at our old Flat T headquarters—that Stump Yole and High Bob Caldwell. They're bad 'uns, that pair. And boy, while you were in town I did a lot of thinkin'. I want you to let this whole damn thing drop. There ain't no sense in fightin' what you can't lick. Like I said before, I'll get along just the way things are. Ain't no part of the deal worth gettin' shot over. Could I see any show of us comin' out on top, then I'd say—go to it! But from here, I can't see no part of such a show.'

'To hear you talk,' scoffed Tracy mildly, 'anybody would think we had nothing on our side. But we have. We got enough to have a good try. If we get licked, at least friend Tasker will know he's been to a waltz. And now I'm off for Comanche Junction.'

Buck jerked erect. 'Comanche Junction! Hell, boy, you just come from there. Why'd you be goin' back?'

Tracy grinned. 'I got some questions to ask. Important ones. And I'm borrowing your horse. Mine could stand a rest.'

Jack Dhu had been eating silently. Now he stirred and spoke.

'Me, I've been lookin' and listenin'. And while I ain't got all the picture, I got some of it. This Tasker Scott seems to shape up as a first class bastard. Maybe we ought to call on him and run him plumb to hell an' gone.'

Tracy's grin became a chuckle. 'Now I'd

expect that reaction from you, Jack. But it's not that simple. Buck is right when he says that Scott is dug in deep. And rooting him out will have to be a little bit at a time.'

'He owns considerable hereabouts?'

'Plenty! And what he doesn't, he claims.'

Jack Dhu wagged his head. 'Just so. I've seen 'em that way in Texas. Ownin' two-thirds of a big county, but not happy unless they can grab off the other third. Now about this ride back to Comanche Junction—'

'Open and shut,' Tracy told him. 'Once there was something like three hundred head of white-faces under the Flat T brand feeding on Maacama Basin grass. Today's there's none. What happened to them? We've Buck's word for it that Tasker Scott rustled them. But where to? Certainly he couldn't keep that many head hid out in the basin. So he must have driven them somewhere for shipment. In which case there'll be a record of it. I'm going to look for that record at Comanche Junction.'

'Scott would have to be mighty sure of himself to pull a deal that broad,' Jack Dhu observed.

'Yes,' agreed Tracy. 'But his kind can turn that way. The bigger they get, the greedier they get, and the more they delude themselves. They believe only what they want to believe, and, sooner or later, they reach too far. Then they get cut down to size.

'Scott figured he had Buck pushed to the wall. And after the way, and for the reason I hauled out of the basin, it was a fair gamble I wouldn't come back. And if I did, that I wouldn't shape up as any great problem, not after the weak show I'd put on before.'

Finished with his meal, Tracy leaned back and built a cigarette.

'Considerable ride to Comanche Junction,' hinted Jack Dhu succinctly. 'Maybe you could use company.'

Tracy shook his head. 'No need, Jack. You stay right here with Buck and take it easy until I get back.'

He added a meaning look to the words which the Texan did not miss. And when Tracy went out to catch and saddle, Jack Dhu followed. At the corral, Tracy explained further.

'After what happened yesterday afternoon and this morning in town, Tasker Scott certainly must realize that I'm set to argue a number of things with him. And because Buck and I were partners before, he might try to hit at me through Buck. In his younger days, Buck could take care of himself in any company, but he's an old dog now and his fangs are considerable worn down. I'd feel mighty bad if anything more happened to him because of me. I'd take it as a big favor if you'd stick around, Jack. Then I won't worry.'

'I like the old feller,' Jack Dhu said briefly. 'I'll be on hand.' He indicated Tracy's lean midriff. 'You're still half naked.'

Tracy grinned. 'Don't worry. I'm going to strap on a gun.'

With a shoulder hitched against a door post of the land office, Rufe Wilkens observed sunset take over this town of Antelope and spread its smoky blue shadows along a street of dwindling activity. His glance, clever and restless, roamed the street, missing nothing of any importance, while his swarthy, coarse-featured face was held with a speculative brooding. Presently he straightened and showed quickening interest as Mark Kenna appeared down street and headed his way.

'Took you long enough,' he grumbled mildly as Kenna came up. He tempered this criticism by leading the way through the land office to the back room, where he produced bottle and glasses from a desk drawer and poured a couple of generous drinks. Lifting his glass, he eyed the whiskey against day's lessening light beyond the window, drank and smacked his heavy lips. 'What luck did you have?'

'For a time it seemed I might have none at all,' Kenna said, pulling up a chair. 'You said not to beat any drums, so I didn't. I played it

85

casual and careful. There are a lot of people in this town now who never heard of anybody named Tracy. I went all up and down the street and met a lot who didn't. That store-keeper, Asa Bingham, he knows Tracy. But he's a tight-mouth, and he shut up quick when I began asking questions. I was about ready to give up when I struck pay dirt. An old roustabout down at the livery corrals admitted that he knew Tracy, but he was kind of tight-mouthed, too, until I bought him a couple of jolts of liquor. After that I could hardly get away from him.'

Kenna paused to savor his own drink and to build one of his husk cigarettes.

'It's quite a story, if we can believe that roustabout, and I believe we can, because it adds in with what we already know about Tracy. Seems when Tracy was here in Maacama Basin before, him and a fellow named Buck Theodore ran a fair-sized cattle spread over toward the Chancellor Peak escarpment somewhere. Tracy and a girl named Lucy Garland were plenty sweet on each other and by all the signs seemed about to make a match of it. Then, of a sudden and for no apparent good reason, the girl up and marries Tasker Scott, and she's Mrs Tasker Scott today. After which, Tracy pulled stakes and left the basin. Everybody figured he was afraid of Scott and that he was gone for good.'

86

'But he wasn't,' murmured Wilkens, filling both glasses again before corking the bottle and putting it back in the desk drawer. 'No, he wasn't afraid of Scott and he wasn't gone for good, for he's very much back among us and by all the signs—though Scott would deny it—has friend Tasker in considerable of a sweat. And I wonder why? That about Scott's wife is interesting, very interesting!'

Wilkens mused over this while carefully spinning his glass around and around between thumb and forefinger.

'Tracy didn't strike me as being much afraid of anything,' supplied Kenna. 'Not by the way he looked and talked when he was in the office, looking over that west side map. And the one with him—now there was a tough one! Here's something to prove it. I heard a couple of wagon men talking. It seems the town marshal tried to slap an arrest on Tracy for some reason. He even threw a gun on him. Then Tracy's partner showed and put a gun on the marshal. Made him drop his weapon, take off his badge and throw it in the street.'

Rufe Wilkens exclaimed softly. 'So that's how it was!'

Startled, Kenna stared. 'That's how what was?'

'Why, on my way back from Scott's office I stopped in at the Trail House for some cigars. This fellow was stacked up against the bar, really taking on the whiskey. Earlier, I'd seen him coming out of Scott's office, wearing a badge. Now he didn't have the badge. And I wondered. Now I know why he was lapping it up at such a rate.'

'Well,' Kenna said, 'there you have it, Rufe. All I could find out and all we know. What does it tell you?'

Wilkens did not answer immediately, instead staring into nothing, again speculating, again brooding. Finally he stirred.

'I think it might be wise to have another good look at things,' he said slowly. 'A good, all-over look! After that, most likely, another and broader understanding with friend Tasker.'

'Because we're afraid of Tracy, too?'

'No,' differed Wilkens, entirely without rancor, 'not scared. Just that we believe in being careful. Oh, damned careful!'

'And the bigger the risk the bigger the pay should be, is that it?' The avarice that gleamed in Mark Kenna's eyes was as swift as the question.

'That's it,' nodded Wilkens dryly. 'Bigger pay. Much bigger!'

CHAPTER SIX

By design, Lee Tracy reached the desert side of Smoky Pass after full sundown. Out ahead, the far rim of the world rioted with an explosion of sunset color and the desert was a sea of layered shades; flame at the top, then a swimming lavender, and finally, against the very earth itself, a twilight blue that held and deepened toward darkness.

The lingering breath of the desert day still cloaked this flank of the Mingo Hills, and Tracy felt the parching dryness of it pull at his cheeks as he dropped to meet the long miles of flatness before him. But he knew that soon a night sky would let down a cooling breath which would preserve the vigor of the horse under him. By the time the sun came up tomorrow morning he would have cut the distance to Comanche Junction by well over a third, and when he reached Vinegar Wells at midday he would be better than halfway to his destination. For though it had taken four days to bring Ben Pardee's horse herd in from Comanche Junction, progress had of necessity been at less than half that of a single rider, lining straight through. Now, with a wisdom gleaned from similar hours under watching stars, Tracy settled to his lonely ride.

At midnight he made halt for an hour, unsaddling and rubbing down his horse, then laying out a feed of oats from the pack behind his saddle cantle. Into a small, fire-blackened pot from the same pack, he poured a measure of water from his canteen, added a handful of coffee, then tucked the pot against a thin blaze of dried sage twigs. When the coffee boiled he set it aside to cool a little, after which he drank straight from the pot, washing down some cold biscuits and a slab of cold venison steak which Buck Theodore had added to his pack. A couple of Durham cigarettes used up the balance of the hour while the fire's scanty coals dwindled to gray nothingness against the earth.

In saddle again, he felt the lift which the rest and feed of oats had given his horse, and so faced the slow, cold, very early morning, when in all the world only a vagrant breath of restless night wind, whispered in the sage, and the watching stars above, seemed awake. Hours later and miles further along, with the first faint streak of light showing in the east, a pair of coyotes, mourning from spots far apart, signaled another night's hunting done with, and the approach of a new dawn.

Presently the deep, unbroken blackness all about him close to the earth began to thin, and objects which the gloom had shrouded

to invisibility, abruptly took on subst
and a quickening identity; a clump of
here, the weathered bones of an ancient
outcrop there. The stars faded and it
day.

He greeted this face with satisfaction,
meant that much of his journey lay be
him. But he made no pause, instead ke
his mount steadily at it, for Vinegar
and water lay out ahead, and with it v
come another rest. The sun lifted abov
now shadow-distant Mingo Hills and
first a welcome warmth, then quick
heat between his shoulders, and night'
shadow left the land. Just short of midd
rode in at Vinegar Wells.

Here was water, frugal and bitter, bu
welcome. Here also a flimsy, brush
shelter, and in the scanty shade of this,
and rider rested through the slu
afternoon, with Tracy managing to cat
hour or two of fitful sleep.

At sundown there was the balance
oats for the horse and another pot of
for Tracy himself. Then once mor
deepening night with its far, lonely,
miles, and finally another dawn and ar
sunrise which saw, lifting out of th
country ahead, a water tower and ta
black iron, the faded yellow of a dumpy
station house, and the low-huddled ou
of a handful of other deeply weat

91

buildings.

North and south, glinting in day's first sunlight, and seemingly reaching from infinity to infinity, ran the railroad's parallel threads of steel, with the spidery lift of telegraph poles marching beside them.

Besides a spread of cattle shipping pens, Comanche Junction's principle reason for existance was as a water stop. Beyond these factors there was only a one-story hotel and eating house of sorts, a dingy general store, a stable, and a short dozen other odd shanties scattered about.

Lee Tracy rode into the runway of the stable, laid a dollar in the palm of a round-faced Shoshone lad of fourteen or fifteen, with orders for the feeding and care of a spent and weary horse, then sought the hotel for food for himself, pausing at the watering trough outside the stable long enough to sluice the desert dust from his parched and tight-drawn cheeks. Overflow from the trough had made its own little bog and here half a dozen blackbirds teetered and strutted, and several swallows fluttered, gathering mud for nests under the stable's ancient eaves.

Late breakfast odors came to Tracy, quickening his saddle-stiffened stride as he tramped over to the hotel. In the dining room a gaunt, thin-faced woman was clearing away an armful of dishes and she

92

paused to eye him with kindly disapproval.
'You again! Set to talk me out of another
free meal?'

Tracy showed a tired grin. 'No, Ma'am.
Going to buy one and pay you for the other.'

She sniffed, the severity of her face
breaking up.

'Now that is a surprise! Never expected to
see you again. That job you were going to get
couldn't have lasted very long.'

'Just to Maacama Basin.'

'And now you're here again, expecting to
find another in this God-forsaken spot? Why
didn't you stay in Maacama Basin? I hear
real big things are going on there.'

'Something like that,' Tracy agreed. 'And
I am going back. After I find out something.'

'Find out what?'

'About cattle shipments.'

'Haven't been any since spring. Won't be
any until maybe next fall. Only a driveling
idiot would try to drive cattle across the
desert at this time of year.'

'I'd figure so,' agreed Tracy again. 'But
the shipments I'm interested in could have
been made last spring, or the fall or spring
before.'

'Then,' declared the thin-faced woman,
'you'll have to see Cass Wiley, the station
agent. And he can be the laziest, most
contrary male critter I know. And I know
plenty of them!'

93

Tracy's grin became a chuckle. 'I'll take your word for it, Ma'am. Now, how's for breakfast?'

Some time later he walked into the station house.

Cass Wiley, the agent, was short, stout and moon-faced. He was brewing a pot of coffee on the station house stove and bent to savor the steamy fragrance of this before coming around.

Tracy leaned on the counter and pointed at the telegraph key.

'How's for calling Jeff Barron at Crestline? You've probably wire-talked with him plenty of times.'

Wiley studied him for a moment. 'Cost you money.'

'So I figured,' Tracy nodded. 'I can stand a dollar or two. So you call Jeff. Ask him if he knows Lee Tracy, and if Tracy is a friend of his.'

Wiley went over to the key and rattled off a station call. Presently answer came back. For a little time Wiley sent and received, every now and then taking another look at his visitor. He was smiling faintly when he signed off and came over to the counter.

'You're Tracy, of course?'

'That's right.'

'Jeff Barron did a pretty fair job of describing you. What's behind all this? Something you want?'

'Yes. It might be against regulations, but I'd sure appreciate it if I could look over some of your past cattle shipping records.'

Wiley considered, then shrugged.

'Jeff said a favor to you would be a favor to him. How far back in the records are you interested?'

'Say a year and a half. Two at the most.'

Wiley lifted several twine-tied bundles of dusty shipping records from a shelf beneath the counter. He glanced at some dates then handed one of the bundles to Tracy. 'Try this one.'

Tracy removed the twine and pored through the contents. Nearing the bottom of the pile he stirred and murmured his satisfaction. Wiley threw him a quick glance.

'What you were looking for?'

'Just!' exulted Tracy. 'Listen to this. One hundred and thirty-four head of Herefords. Primary brand, Flat T. Vented to Lazy Dollar. Consigned to Gimball & Reese, Kansas City. Shipped by—T. R. Scott.'

Wiley frowned, puzzled.

'What's so interesting there? All perfectly regular.'

'Except for one thing,' stated Tracy bluntly. 'To my certain knowledge, T. R. Scott never bought and paid for a single head of Flat T cattle in his life!'

'Hell you say! You mean—that Flat T stuff was rustled?'

'Is there any other word for it? Certainly none of it was ever given or sold to him.'

Definite worry showed in Wiley's expression. 'That puts me in a bad spot, a damn bad spot!'

'Not unless you knew the cattle were rustled,' soothed Tracy. 'Which of course you didn't.'

'Had no slightest idea,' said Wiley. 'In my time I've shipped plenty of vented brands that were legitimate. I figured that shipment the same. Any more like it?'

In the first bundle there were no more, but in the next there was another invoice covering a like shipment, straight Flat T, vented to Lazy Dollar, along with two others listing mixed shipments of legitimate Lazy Dollar and Flat T, vented. All consigned to the same destination, all shipped by T. R. Scott.

Tracy did a little mental arithmetic, then leaned back, nodding. 'Comes out about right in numbers.' He gave the four invoices to Wiley. 'You got a place you can put these where nobody but you can get at them?'

Wiley indicated the squat iron safe against the far wall.

'Ancient equipment, but still sound.'

Tracy built a cigarette. 'I don't want to bring trouble down on you. But when the fire begins to really burn, Mister T. R. Scott could have a try at getting hold of those invoices. And be pretty desperate about it.'

Of a sudden, Cass Wiley's round, moon face seemed leaner, harder. He glanced at a Winchester racked on the wall behind the stove.

'That's useful as well as ornamental,' he said succinctly. 'And I think I'd enjoy throwing down on this fellow Scott for making a sucker of me. Don't worry. Should you want to see them again, the invoices will be right here!'

Deeply weary, Tracy yawned and stretched. 'You've been mighty decent about this, friend.' He smiled. 'Kinda more than I expected.'

Wiley chuckled. 'That suggests you've been listening to Maude Kemper, over at the hotel. Maude loves to scorch the hides of all men, particularly fusty old bachelors like me. But behind the scolding is one of the biggest hearts I know. Maude's our first citizen. Here in Comanche Junction we wouldn't know what to do without her.'

Tracy reached for his pocket. 'The telegraph call—how much do I owe you?'

'Not a dime,' Wiley declared. 'You've really done me and the railroad a favor. Scott comes out of Maacama Basin, doesn't he?'

Tracy nodded. 'My stamping ground, too.'

'Then I could see you again, one of these days. There's talk the railroad may build a branch into Maacama Basin. Should that happen, I might draw the agent job there.'

At the door Tracy paused. 'How real is the talk?'

'At the moment, just gossip,' Wiley said. 'But I've been around long enough to know that when gossip of new construction hangs on and on, something generally comes of it.'

Tracy stretched and yawned again. Observing, Cass Wiley asked, 'When you heading back to Maacama?'

Tracy considered briefly. 'At sundown. Right now I'm for a corner where I can sleep until then.'

Wiley jerked an indicating head. 'Most generally I stay at Maude Kemper's hotel. But when outfits from the Lyle Fork and Red Prairie and Maacama Basin are shipping, trains are making up at all hours, day and night. So I have to stick close, and between runs I catch a few winks in that back room yonder. You're welcome to the bunk there.'

'Man, you're too generous,' Tracy protested.

'Jeff Barron said to treat you right, didn't he?'

The back room was small, practically bare except for the bunk, and the mattress on this was thin and lumpy. But to Tracy it was cloud-like.

Weary as he was, sleep was elusive, as the significance of what he had uncovered kept turning over and over in his mind. Here were facts to damage Tasker Scott greatly, and it was hard to understand how the man could have left such record of bare-faced villainy behind him. Nothing could more greatly emphasize an inate ruthlessness, nor a confidence in strength and position and invulnerability.

Bleakness colored Lee Tracy's thoughts. Despite the odds, that ruthlessness would be challenged, the strength and position tested.

These things finally decided, inner tumult quieted and sleep took over.

*   *   *

Back in Maacama Basin, Tasker Scott left his office precisely at half-past five in the afternoon. This was his daily habit, with his first stop at the Trail House bar where he leisurely poured two drinks from a private bottle and as leisurely consumed them, along with a cigar, thus using up a half hour of time. Not because he particularly enjoyed the atmosphere of the Trail House, nor the company of those who patronized it. But here, toward the end of the day men gathered to drink and make talk.

It was this talk which interested Scott and the major reason for his presence in the place. Standing quietly at the far end of the bar, concerned apparently only with the drink in front of him and the cigar which burned between his teeth, he missed little of what went on around him. He listened to the talk, winnowed what he heard, discarding that which was meaningless or of no account to him, while making the most of all worth his concern. It was his way of keeping his finger on the pulse of the basin; testing its over-all temper and judging how the tides of men's thoughts and desires were running.

It pleased him to do this much as a monarch might test his kingdom and the temper of his subjects, for the complex of need for power and ownership ran strong in Tasker Scott and colored virtually his every move. Long ago had he set out to, within all possible limits, make of this Maacama Basin his kingdom, and by any means necessary to the end. Where cajolery and trickery would get him what he wanted, he did not hesitate to use such. Where scheming would serve, he schemed. Where thievery served, he stole. And where violence was necessary, he would call on it.

He stood a tall man, padded somewhat with the excess flesh of rich living. His florid good looks were marred only by the hardness about his eyes and a suggestion of predatory ruthlessness when his face was viewed in profile. His mouth was the main betraying feature here, full-lipped with a curl to it as though beyond it lay an inward sneer which saw all other men as lesser beings.

In the talk about him he listened for the mention of one name. That of Lee Tracy. And knew a certain relief when he heard none. For he had grown uneasy about Lee Tracy. Here was a man he had believed he was forever done with, one who would never again be of any consequence in his affairs. In this he had been wrong. Lee Tracy was back in Maacama Basin and showing a side to his makeup unsuspected and definitely disquieting. A tough side.

Behind narrowed, thoughtful eyes, Scott reviewed certain events which followed Tracy's reappearance in the basin. Mainly how he had probed certain land office records and questioned them. And how, before that, when they had faced each other on the day of Tracy's reappearance, he had been cool and easy and tauntingly defiant. And finally, how he and a lank Texan companion had made a joke of Ben Pardee as town marshal.

Scott tightened his teeth on his cigar and threw a glance toward a far corner of the barroom where, slumped beside a poker table, head on a limply flung arm, Ben Pardee snored in drunken sleep, still working on alcohol to hide his shame.

Again Scott set down on his cigar, and this time, bitten cleanly off, the perfecto fell from his lips. He spat out the mangled tip of it, met the bartender's startled glance with a hard stare, flung a dollar on the bar and stamped out. Through the first of sunset shadows he went down street to the livery stable.

A grizzled stable hand was waiting for him, leading out a powerful, short-coupled blue roan, already bridled and under saddle. As Scott took the rein, the old fellow, mildly garrulous, made casual inquiry.

'How long's Lee Tracy been back in the basin, Mr Scott?'

Scott's glance was quick and intent. 'Tracy! He been around here today?'

'Not that I know of. But I hear some talk. And then, one of them fellers from the land office tackled me and wanted to know all about him. Like Tracy was somebody important—real important.'

Scott pulled his glance away but was still carefully attentive.

'What kind of talk did you hear, Rooney? About Tracy, I mean.'

The stable hand shrugged. 'That he's come back a damn lot tougher than when he left. That he licked a feller named Pardee, and the next day, when this Pardee made a play at arrestin' him from behind a marshal's badge, Tracy and a friend of his made Pardee back down, took his gun away from him and threw his badge out into the street. That sure ain't the kind of Tracy who used to be in these parts.'

Tasker Scott considered a moment before toeing his stirrup and swinging up. The roan had spirit and began to shift and fiddle, but was set back sharply.

'Which one of the men from the land office was asking the questions?'

'Not the main feller. The other one, the fancy-actin' one.'

'And he wanted to know about Tracy?'

'That's right, he sure did.'

'What did you tell him?'

'All the different things I knew.' Old Jeb Rooney began to swell his narrow chest importantly, then, glimpsing the tightening of Tasker Scott's cheeks, hastily added, 'No reason why I shouldn't have, was there?'

Tasker Scott stared off toward the open basin country.

'No reason at all. Thanks for letting me know.'

He gave the roan its head and it lifted immediately to a fast trot. Jeb Rooney squinted after Scott's receding back, then shuffled away to his evening chores.

Leaving town, Tasker Scott headed directly east along the well-marked trail which led to Lazy Dollar headquarters. A fairly active man, the confinement of office work irked him and he looked forward to his ride home through the evening coolness and the quickening dusk.

Across the miles, the southern end of the Chancellor Peak escarpment was a long-running, down-slanting barrier, building up with shadow, while to the north the upper reaches of the peak itself still held the last of the sun and stood like an island thrusting up from a sea of powder-blue mists. Scott's glance, touching the peak, held there, and in sudden decision he reined away from the home trail and laid an angling course toward the darkening base of the peak.

Later, in the full dark, he struck Border Creek some quarter mile below Flat T, and marking the spark of light in the ranchhouse which told of the ranch's occupancy, he swung that way, sending the roan up the slope at a jog, the muffled thump of driving hoofs carrying ahead of him.

On closer approach the spark of light became the square of a window, and now also showed the yellow rectangle of a swiftly opened and closed door. During this small interval a man stepped into the outer dark and his challenge hit with a droning harshness.

'You out there, name yourself!'

Scott hauled up and gave answer. 'Tasker Scott.'

A muttered exclamation of surprise was followed by a more mollified tone.

'Light and come on in.'

Scott swung down, ground reined the roan

and stepped into a room thick with an accumulation of rancid odors. Supper had been recently cooked and eaten and the table was littered with unwashed dishes, some from the just finished meal, others left from past use. Brown paper cigarette butts littered table and floor. A frying pan, overlong on a too-hot stove, gave off the acridity of badly scorched bacon grease. A lamp with a wick in need of trimming and adjustment flickered badly, sooting up its chimney and adding the raw and biting break of kerosene fumes to the room's murkiness. Finally, underlying all these olfactory offenses and by far the worst, lurked the stench of unwashed humans and of their stale sweat.

Tasker Scott looked around, his lips curling with disgust. His remark fell bitingly.

'Don't tell me you fellows like to live this way?'

The squat, pock-marked man still at the table, spooned sugar copiously into a gummy coffee cup and grunted lazily. 'What's wrong with it?'

'It's a damned pigsty!' asserted Scott flatly.

Now the high and stringy one who had challenged Scott's approach, swung restlessly.

'If it suits Stump and me, why should you care? Did you ride plumb out here to tell us that?'

'No,' said Scott, 'I didn't.'

He paused, measuring these two. Stump Yole, there at the table. And High Bob Caldwell, here beside him. Dirty they were, and uncouth. Greedy. Stupid in many ways, but weasel sly in others. Brutal, and without vestige of conscience. Dangerous as a pair of sluggish, venom-charged rattlesnakes. All these things they were, and therefore useful to a man driven by ambitious, unscrupulous purpose. Scott covered up his disgust.

'There's a chore that needs doing.'

'What kind of a chore?' demanded Stump Yole.

To ward off the worst of the offensive atmosphere, Scott got out a cigar and lit it, mouthing the smoke with relish.

'That fellow living in the line camp by the timber burn north of here—I want you to run him out.'

'Could be somebody with him,' High Bob Caldwell said in his thin, complaining way.

'Somebody with him! How's that?'

'Feller was by yesterday, wantin' to know about a Buck Theodore. So Stump and me, we sent him along to the line camp.'

Tasker Scott's lips tightened about his cigar. 'That wasn't smart.'

High Bob blinked. 'Why wasn't it? Old feller at the line camp is named Theodore, ain't he?'

Scott waved an impatient hand. 'All right,

all right! What did this one asking for Theodore, look like?'

'Young feller, but not too young. And, well—' High Bob shrugged. 'Knew how to sit a horse.'

'He give you his name?'

'No, and we never asked him. He said he was a friend of Buck Theodore, that's all.'

'Well, if he's still there,' Tasker Scott said tightly, 'run him out, too.'

High Bob's eyes narrowed in speculation. 'A chance they might not run, not easy. They don't, how rough you want me and Stump to get?'

'As rough as you have to.'

High Bob looked at Stump Yole. Stump smiled blandly, his eyes turning sly.

'Could be, should things turn real rough, Bob or me could get a little hurt. Stop a load of buckshot, or something like that. And when a feller risks his skin, he ought to be paid good. Bob and me, we can always use a few extra dollars.'

Tasker Scott stared from one to the other with a swift-rising anger.

'What the hell are you talking about, Yole? Since I hired you two on, all you've had to do is lay around out here and sleep and eat. Now, the first time I ask more of you than that, you start talking more money. Well, you're out of luck!'

'Why then,' said Stump, 'maybe Bob and

107

me just ain't interested in this chore.'

Scott didn't retreat an inch. 'Then you'll get the hell out of here! Go find somebody else willing to pay you and feed you for doing nothing.'

Stump Yole climbed slowly to his feet, to stand on inordinately short and bowed legs, which held up an equally inordinately long torso; a physical imbalance which gave him a simian look that had made more than one man back away. He was calculating the same result now on Tasker Scott.

'Maybe Bob and me, we don't feel like clearing out of here. Then what?'

Abruptly Tasker Scott's face was just as heavy and brutal as that of this grotesquely built man facing him. And there was neither hesitancy or indecisiveness in the ultimatum laid down.

'You know what's good for you, you'll be out of here by morning. You heard me—by morning!'

With this, Scott turned to the door, but paused at Stump Yole's placating words.

'Hell, I was just tryin' to horse-trade a little, Mr Scott.'

'When I give orders, I don't bargain,' rapped Scott shortly. 'I've fired better men than you'll ever be!'

Stump Yole's expression was strictly bland again.

'First thing in the morning, Bob and me'll

take care of that chore, Mr Scott.'

Tasker Scott fought back his anger. 'All right. But don't ever try to bargain with me again. I don't like it!'

Then he was gone, cigar smoke trailing across his shoulder. The roan's quick hoofs sent back departing echoes. High Bob Caldwell looked at his partner accusingly.

'You backed down, Stump. You should have stayed with him. He'd have come across.'

Stump Yole shook his head. 'No he wouldn't. He's tougher than we figgered. And we ain't got a good hold on him yet. Later on, when we have, then you'll see!'

CHAPTER SEVEN

Leaving Flat T, Tasker Scott rode directly homeward, but this break in his usual habit had used up a couple of hours. By the time he pulled in at Lazy Dollar headquarters the stars were high and bright. A slow current of night wind seeping down from the Chancellor Peak escarpment brought the chill of lofty country with it.

Lazy Dollar was a big spread. It had been so when Hack Garland was alive, and since taking over after Hack's death, Tasker Scott had added to it in the way of more corrals and feed sheds, another barn and a new and larger bunkhouse. Not that there was any crying need for these new additions, but it pleased him to thus assert his influence and authority. Also, it fitted in with his long range plans for the future, which would see him growing ever more powerful in Maacama Basin through possession.

Lights shone yellow in the ranchhouse and the new bunkhouse. A cigarette tip glowed by the cavvy corral and as Scott pulled up there, this tip spun earthwards and went out in a tiny explosion of sparks. A shadowy figure moved forward to take over the roan's rein and a soft drawl struck upwards.

'Must have been a busy day, Mr Scott. Held you over later than usual.'

'Yes,' said Scott, swinging down. 'That's it, Lonnie.' He glanced toward the dark sprawl of the ranchhouse with its several glowing windows. 'Mrs Scott got company?'

'No, sir,' said Lonnie Raikes. 'Not that I know of. You'll want the roan at the regular time tomorrow?'

'That's it,' Scott said. 'The regular time.'

He crossed to the ranchhouse, letting himself in at a side door which opened into the ranch office. Here it was dark. But he knew the layout of the room thoroughly and soon had a lamp going. He hung his hat and coat on a wall peg, then passed through an inner door into the main run of the

110

ranchhouse.

Before a wide hearth of native stone in the long, low-ceilinged living room, Lucy Scott was curled in an armchair, staring at the fire. She looked up briefly at her husband's entrance, then returned her gaze to the flicker of the flames. She did not speak. Scott swung his shoulders and made testy observation.

'With so many lights burning I thought there might be a celebration brewing. Though I wouldn't know what for. Or were you expecting company?'

Again she looked at him. 'Company! What company? Who, for instance, would likely visit Lazy Dollar now?' Again she stared at the flames, her face brooding. 'There's nothing in this house any more. Maybe I lit the lights just to pretend there was.'

Scott's irritation deepened. 'You talk like a child, a spoiled one. What, or who, would you pretend was here?'

'My father. I miss him. I'm just realizing how much I miss him. In his way he was good to me. And I paid him back by selling him out to you.' She choked up and turned her head fully away, blinking rapidly.

'Now I will be damned!' ejaculated Scott. 'Would you be growing sentimental at this stage of the game?'

She did not answer, keeping her head averted while reaching for a handkerchief.

Scott took a turn up and down the room, and when he spoke again his tone was a trifle more mild.

'What's over with and past is over with and past. Weeping won't bring it back. Plainly speaking, your father was a damned old scorpion, who figured that by adding me to the family he was just upping his hand a little more. And he used you to get me. But he never fooled me on that angle. And when he found he couldn't handle me, you might say he bit himself and died of his own poison. One thing is certain—he's no man to waste tears over.'

Anger dried Lucy Scott's eyes. She came around and to her feet all in one motion.

'You're a thorough, callous brute, aren't you?'

He laughed shortly and without mirth. 'That's better. Now I recognize you again. But that droopy, weepy thing of a minute ago—'

He paused in his pacing, reaching for her. She eluded him, put the chair between them.

'Don't touch me!' she flared. 'Don't ever touch me again. Either in anger—or otherwise!'

He stared, a little incredulous. 'What kind of nonsense is this?'

'No nonsense. Just fact!'

They matched glances, hers defiant and stormy, his puzzled and touched with baffled anger. There was no denying her dark beauty, or misreading the aversion in her expression. And the one held him as it always had, while the other goaded him. His first impulse was to get hold of her, shake her, rough her up a little as he had in his town office yesterday. But something told him such tactics would not serve now. It were better to try and talk her out of this mood. He took another turn about the room.

'Let's come back to common sense, Lucy. This is what we both wanted. And—'

'This!' she broke in scornfully.

'You know what I mean,' he said impatiently. 'We set out to grow big, you and I. So big we could just about run this damn basin to suit ourselves. We made those plans together and we acted on them. They've brought us a long way and they'll take us a lot farther if we stay with them. They'll take us to where we want to get. So let's quit this damn haggling and quit playing the mournful hypocrite. You knew what you wanted the same as I knew what I wanted. And we're both getting what we wanted.'

'No,' she differed, very definitely. 'No, we're not. Maybe you are, but I'm not.'

He stopped before her again, the mood he had first brought into the room, returning.

'Just what in hell do you want?'

'Not what I thought I did. Certainly not a home as empty of, of all the things that make a home, as this place. Or—or—'

'Or a husband you no longer give a damn for. Would that be it?' Scott suggested caustically.

She looked at him steadily for a moment before slowly nodding.

'As long as you ask, yes. Yes, that is it. One I neither care for nor respect.'

Inwardly, Scott squirmed. This struck at two of the major factors in his makeup, his ego and his sense of possession, both of which were more or less founded on vanity. And here was voiced a flat statement of fact which sliced that vanity to ribbons. It was entirely like him to refuse to accept the fact.

'Now you're really talking foolish. I don't think you really mean that. Tomorrow you'll feel different.'

'No,' she said, in that steady, distinct way. 'Not tomorrow. Not ever!'

He considered her, his jaw tightly clamped, his lips pulling thin.

'So you'd be a quitter,' he accused. 'That's it—a quitter. We made a bargain, you and me. I've kept my part of it. I've reached for and got a lot of things we both agreed we wanted. If I've had to be rough about it in places, well—that was part of the bargain, of the agreement. The agreement that you'd ride with me all the way. Results were what we were interested in, not methods. Or ethics either, for that matter.

And now you'd try and snivel out.'

'Call it what you wish,' she shrugged. 'I simply know I'm in no way proud of what we have or how we've gotten it. And after all is said and done, we really have nothing. Nothing that counts.'

He stared past her, the muscles at his jaw corners bunching and working, his hands clenching and unclenching.

'It's Tracy, isn't it? Up until you knew he was back, you were all you had agreed to be. Yeah, of course it's Tracy.'

She did not answer and Scott brought his glance back to her.

'All right. We know exactly how we stand. Up to a point. I'll make the rest of it very clear, so you can make no mistake about it. You're my wife. Don't ever forget that fact for one little minute. Which means you're subject to my authority and you'll do as you're told. I'm telling you, now. Stay away from Lee Tracy.'

'You've said that before,' Lucy Scott retorted. 'I don't think you need worry. Lee Tracy wouldn't wipe his feet on either of us. And who can blame him?'

'Just so you know,' insisted Tasker Scott. 'Stay away from him! I'll take care of Mister Tracy. Now I'll have my supper.'

Lucy resumed her chair and study of the fire. 'You'll have to get it somewhere else than in this house. I didn't cook any.'

Face twisted with anger, Tasker Scott spun away and stamped back into the ranch office, there to don hat and coat again before making his way through the dark to the cook-shack and a late meal.

*　　*　　*

Lee Tracy rode through Smoky Pass to face a sun new risen beyond the distant, blue-misted shoulders of Chancellor Peak. Gray desert dust powdered man and horse and Tracy was fine drawn from the long saddle miles. But glimpse of Maacama Basin and the breath of the river lifted some of the saddle weariness from his shoulders. As he drifted down the long, winding coulee to the river flats his glance searched for the John Vail camp.

It was right where it had been, but with a difference. Now the clutter of gear that had been stacked around, waiting permanent placement, had been loaded back in the wagon. Except for a small fire about which Mrs Vail, Kip and the two younger children were gathered at breakfast, the camp was completely cleaned up. At the wagon, John Vail had his heavy team, harnessing them. His manner, as Tracy rode up, was half welcome, half resentful.

Tracy looked around. 'Don't tell me you're pulling out?'

John Vail jerked a nod. 'That's it.'

'Why? What's wrong?'

'This land has already been filed on.'

'Who says so?'

'The land office,' John Vail growled. 'And I saw the map to prove it. So—' He shrugged heavily.

'Did they tell you who filed on it?' Tracy persisted.

Vail shrugged again. 'Didn't ask. Wouldn't have changed things or done any good, anyhow. The record's there. On the map. I saw it. Nothing I can do about it now.'

'Don't be too sure of that,' Tracy cautioned quietly. 'I saw that same map. When I asked who had filed on the land they didn't want to tell me. But I got it out of them. Tasker Scott had done the filing. Well, look around. Do you see any sign of occupancy or development work? No, and I don't either. Yet the law specifies both occupancy and development requirements be complied with to make a homestead claim legal and binding. It's none of my business, of course, but I think you're making a mistake in moving out.'

The granger buckled a set of hames about the collar of one of his horses before answering. Then he looked up, eyeing Tracy narrowly.

'You're still holding to that railroad idea?'

117

'In part,' Tracy admitted. 'But that isn't all. This is good land we're on. You thought so in the first place or you'd never have stopped here. In your boots I certainly wouldn't leave until I'd seen plenty of better proof that somebody else had fairer claim to it.'

John Vail considered a moment, then slowly shook his head.

'I ain't big enough to fight the land office and its records. Man could get into trouble, doing that. And I can't afford to get into no trouble. I got a family to look after.'

Tracy knew a vague drift of anger. How in hell could any man truly look after the best interests of his family unless he fought for them? Running away from possible trouble never really provided any answers. Of all men, he, Lee Tracy, should know that. Besides, even a man with a family could afford to test the true measure of possible trouble before admitting it as such.

He pushed a hand tiredly across his face and shook his head as though to free it from the bite of his thoughts.

Now to him came the enticing breath of breakfast food, the fragrance of frying bacon and the steaming goodness of hot coffee, and these things pulled his glance to the fire.

Kip Vail was erect, looking at him. She smiled.

'When did you eat last, Mr Tracy?'

'Long enough ago to make it seem like days instead of hours.'

'Why then,' declared the girl simply, 'you must eat again—and now!'

'Of course,' seconded Mrs Vail vigorously. 'We have plenty.'

John Vail added his gruff approval. 'Sure, friend, light and eat.'

Tracy went to the river's edge first, there to water his thirst-fretted horse and to wash away the worst of the desert's dust. He knew some dismay at the whiskery roughness of his cheeks, but there was no help for that. He went back to the fire, dropped on his heels there and accepted a plate of bacon and biscuits and the cup of coffee Kip Vail poured for him.

The warm, savory food was like a jolt of liquor in his clamoring stomach. It lifted him and took some of fatigue's hard tension out of him. Plate and cup were swiftly empty and Kip filled both again. He looked at her and drawled softly.

'Here and there along the trail a man does meet up with an occasional break of luck.'

The remark was innocuous enough, but behind it lay a deeper meaning, as Tracy had intended and which Kip Vail did not miss. As their glances met and held, her eyes took on a deep shining and when she turned away her lips were curved with gentle smiling and her throat and cheeks flushed with more

119

than fire warmth.

John Vail left off harnessing his team to tramp over to the fire, take a cup of coffee from his wife and frown speculatively past the rim of it.

'Confound it, Tracy,' he grumbled, 'you've made me uncertain. I had my mind all set to move on. Now, I don't know.'

Finishing a final mouthful, Tracy got to his feet and built a cigarette.

'I'd never want any trouble to come to you or yours, Mr Vail. At the same time, if the decision was mine, I'd stay right here. For if anyone does happen to have really legitimate prior claim to the land, they can do no more than order you off. Until that happens, I'd stay and have a real try at making my claim stick.'

Vail's concern deepened. He turned to his wife.

'Mama, if it was left to you, what would you do?'

Rachel Vail had ridden the wagon with her man many a weary mile, searching for the one spot she could forever call home. Nor had she ever complained. Sun and wind had punished her face, work and hardship roughened her hands. She had borne children and had her dreams for them. And all these vital elements of life and living had toughened her without upsetting a motherly sweetness and balance. She looked around

120

her and slowly spoke.

'This is a fair land, John Vail. And a body does grow mortal weary, searching for such. I could build my home where I stand and never ask for better. If we have true right here, then I would never give it up, come what may!'

'It could be a lonely fight,' warned John Vail. 'You notice we're the only camp set up along this particular stretch. Other folks believe what the land office records say, and want no part of trouble.'

'It doesn't matter to me what others think,' Rachel Vail said quietly. 'All that counts is the right. With it on our side, nothing else matters.'

John Vail studied her, his expression softening.

'Always,' he said fondly, 'you have more real courage than anyone I ever knew, man or woman. So be it. We stay!'

'Ma'am,' exclaimed Lee Tracy to Mrs Vail, 'I salute you! And thank you for a meal that saved my life. Also, you won't be making this fight alone; you'll have neighbors.'

He smiled at the two shy, big-eyed youngsters, then went to his horse. His final glance was all for Kip Vail, and to her he tipped his hat. After which, as he rode away, crossing the river at a shallows before turning north, he carried the mental picture of her with him.

* * *

At the line camp cabin by the old timber burn, north of Chancellor Peak, Buck Theodore and Jack Dhu were finishing breakfast, a meal leisurely cooked and as leisurely eaten, for just now, time was something they had more of than anything else. They had nothing to do but wait for Lee Tracy to get back from Comanche Junction, and while mixing up the breakfast biscuits, Buck had hazarded the guess that today could see Tracy's return.

'Shouldn't take him long to learn all worth knowin' about that place. Includin' the name and date of birth of everybody there. Wouldn't surprise me none to have him come joggin' in any time now.'

Spinning up an after-breakfast smoke, Jack Dhu nodded, then quickly tipped a listening head.

'Sounds like you called it, Buck. Somebody's showin'.'

As he spoke, the Texan pushed to his feet, crossed to the door and stepped out. And went completely still. Two riders swung to a stop before him. He had never laid eyes on either of them before, but from casual talk Buck Theodore had made he knew instantly who they were.

Stump Yole and High Bob Caldwell.

Stump was the nearer of the two and he laid a six-shooter across the horn of his saddle, the muzzle steadily on Jack Dhu, whose own gun hung on a wall peg in the cabin. The Texan's eyes chilled as his cheeks pulled tight.

'Just what in hell's the idea?' he demanded.

Stump Yole's grin was mocking and it was evil. 'Where you're concerned it's stay just as you are.' He wagged the threatening gun. Then he called to his companion. 'All right, Bob, see who's inside.'

High Bob Caldwell dropped quickly from his saddle, drew a gun and went inside. Buck Theodore had heard the murmur of voices outside, but had gotten none of the import of what had been said. Now rising to his feet, he stared in blank surprise at the intruder facing him. High Bob Caldwell waved his gun.

'You, over against the wall!'

Buck Theodore did not argue. He did as he was told, blinking his wonderment.

'I don't get this. What do you want? If it's a holdup, you'll get damn little for your trouble.'

'Never mind about that,' High Bob shot back. 'Just do as you're told!'

High Bob's glance, searching the cabin swiftly, located Buck's rifle and Jack Dhu's belt gun. These he gathered in then called out.

'Only the old one in here, Stump.'

'Any guns?' Stump asked.

'A couple, and I got those.'

'Fair enough. Bring the old feller out.'

High Bob jerked his head. 'You heard,' he told Buck Theodore.

Buck moved through the door, looked at Stump Yole, then at Jack Dhu, then at Yole again.

'Maybe you can tell us what this is all about?'

'Sure,' said Stump easily. 'You're huntin' other quarters. Livin' here ain't healthy any more.' Now he studied Jack Dhu more closely. 'This ain't the one who asked about you the other day. Where is he?'

'If you mean Lee Tracy, he's not here just now. What do you want with him?'

'Just to tell him he ain't stayin' here, either.' Stump maintained his full attention on Jack Dhu, for there was a cold and savage anger surging in the Texan which Yole did not miss. 'All those ideas you're playin' with, friend—you better forget complete. You try makin' a break, it'll be your last. You hear me!'

Buck Theodore added his word of caution. 'Easy does it, Jack—easy!' He considered a moment, then looked at Stump Yole again.

'This ain't somethin' you figgered out on your own, for you had no cause to. This is bein' done at Tasker Scott's order. Right?'

'Does it matter?' jibed Stump, his heavy, pock-marked face again pulled into a mocking grin. 'Makes no difference either way. You're leavin'.' He lifted his voice. 'Throw their hats out, Bob.'

High Bob Caldwell obeyed literally. After which Stump Yole nodded toward the corral. 'Your broncs are there, your saddles are there. Get goin'!'

'Where to?' Buck demanded.

'Any damn place but here. Move out. And don't come back!'

Buck picked up both hats, donned his, handed over Jack Dhu's. 'All right, Jack,' he said.

Jack Dhu had his fixed look at Stump Yole, and then at High Bob Caldwell, who stood in the cabin doorway.

'It'll be easy to remember you two,' he said softly. 'Real easy. And I will!'

'While you're goin' to get yourself in a real tough fix, just you keep talkin',' retorted Stump Yole, of a sudden all heavy, threatening brute.

Buck Theodore reached for the Texan's arm. 'Come on, Jack,' he urged. 'Nothin's worth that kind of trouble. Come on!'

They caught up and saddled the two horses in the corral and rode away without

125

looking back, old Buck hunched and discouraged, Jack Dhu seething. They passed the little swamp where the blackbirds swayed on the reed tops and the killdeer ran along the shoreline, crying plaintively. In the far distance they reached the river and turned south along this, each caught up in the silent bitterness of his own thoughts. They came finally to Border Creek and broke through the willow thickets which shrouded it. And on the far side saw Lee Tracy riding toward them.

The moment Tracy saw them he knew that something was wrong. He could tell from the way they sat their saddles, and he sent the roan quickly ahead. On closer approach he shed some of his first surge of worry, for neither Buck or Jack Dhu showed any sign of physical injury. Yet, plainly, all was not well, for the Texan's face was hard and drawn and a cold, boiling anger was banked in his eyes.

'All right,' Tracy greeted. 'Something's happened. What?'

'You're looking at the world's greatest damn fool!' The words broke harshly from Jack Dhu. 'They made me look like a puling, bald-faced kid. By God, they did! And I had to take it. I let you down, Tracy, I let you down.'

'No!' differed Buck Theodore. 'No, you didn't, Jack. You let nobody down. You had no idea what them fellers wanted when they rode up. You had no cause to step out ready for war. So they got the drop on you and after that there wasn't anything you could do except what you were told. I had a better chance than you did, but somehow I jest couldn't think or act fast enough. Don't you blame yourself for nothin'. Wasn't your fault, nohow.'

'All right,' Tracy said again. 'Now that I got that much, what's the rest? Just what in hell did happen?'

'They ran us out. And—'

'They?' cut in Tracy. 'Who are they?'

'Stump Yole and High Bob Caldwell,' explained Buck. 'Them two hardcases Tasker Scott's had holdin' down our old Flat T headquarters. Jack and me, we'd jest finished eatin' breakfast. We heard a horse comin' in. Only there was two of them. For all we knew it might have been you. Anyhow, Jack stepped to the door to see who it was and they put a gun on him.'

'I should have made a break,' Jack Dhu said bleakly. 'I should have taken a chance.'

'And got your head shot off,' old Buck said. 'Which wouldn't have done anybody any good. No, they had you dead to rights, and you were smart not tryin' to push your luck.'

'So after that?' prompted Tracy.

Buck shrugged gaunt, tired shoulders.

'They told us to get out of the line camp and stay out. They jest run us off. They let us take our broncs and saddles and that's all.'

'They took our guns,' Jack Dhu brooded. 'But somewhere I'll round me up another, and then all I ask is to meet up with them two bully boys where it's a reasonable even shake. That's all I want, just an even shake!'

'It's no use,' said Buck slowly, shaking a grizzled head. 'Like I been sayin' right along, Tasker Scott's too big for us. He's got too much backin' in men and money. There ain't nothin' in this damn basin worth either of you fellers gettin' killed over. Me, I don't count. I'm too damned far along the trail to count. But I'd feel mortal bad was either of you to get hurt. No, it jest ain't worth tryin' to fight Scott. Ain't nothin' we can do to hurt him, and unless we can hurt him, plenty, we can't lick him.'

'Maybe we can hurt him, Buck,' Tracy observed carefully. 'Maybe we can hurt him—and bad!'

Jack Dhu, beginning to come out of the worst of his anger, showed Tracy a quick glance.

'At Comanche Junction you struck a little gold?'

'I think so. Friend Tasker has made some mistakes. Some bad ones. He's taken too much for granted, and grown careless. Oh, we can hurt him all right. Listen to this.'

Tracy told of Comanche Junction and the information written so indelibly on four shipping invoices.

'It figured up just a little short of three hundred head of vented Flat T white-faces,' he ended. 'Two hundred and eighty-seven to be exact. Which checks pretty close to what you figured you lost, doesn't it, Buck?'

'Close enough,' nodded Buck. 'And you're tellin' us that Scott had the damned gall to ship under his own name?'

'That's it. I saw the invoices. I talked with the station agent.'

'And consigned to Gimball & Reese in Kansas City,' Buck marveled, still finding it hard to believe. 'They're square buyers, Gimball & Reese. They couldn't have been in on it.'

'Of course not. They had no reason to suspect anything wrong, no more than Cass Wiley, the station agent did. They had no way of knowing they were buying stolen cattle.'

'But they were stolen, all right,' Buck growled. 'Every single damn head. I sure never sold Scott any.'

'Which is the point that can cut his heart out,' observed Tracy with some grimness. 'He can't deny the evidence in the shipping invoices, or the testimony of Wiley, the agent, should we need it. And he can't produce a single bill of sale to prove legitimate ownership. He doesn't know it yet, but Mister Scott is in considerable of a bind.'

'It would seem so,' agreed Jack Dhu dryly. 'But we ain't exactly runnin' free and in the clear, ourselves. We're down to our clothes, our saddles and our broncs.' He eyed the Colt gun slung to Tracy's waist. 'And one lone six-shooter. Maybe you better let me have that, Lee. Without braggin', I think I savvy a short gun some better than you.'

'I'm sure of it, Jack,' Tracy said. 'But you'll soon have one of your own again. And we'll have an outfit, too. We'll have to siwash it for a while, but it's the right season of the year for that. Maybe it will turn out to be a good thing to be out of the line camp. Because now everything will be in the open. We know exactly where we stand with Mister Scott.'

Old Buck, still somewhat bewildered by it all, pushed a vague hand across his face.

'What you aimin' to do, Lee? Like Jack says, all we got to our names is jest what you see us with. So where do we start?'

'Over by Smoky Pass,' Tracy told him. 'We're going to stake out some homestead claims. On ground the land office shows is already claimed by Tasker Scott. After we set our corners, we're for town and the land office, where we file and set the records straight. That will be our first good bite out of Tasker Scott's hide, and we'll be strictly within the law while we do it. We'll get around to the stolen cattle deal later.'

'Me,' said Jack Dhu slowly, 'I ain't never owned a foot of ground in my life. Maybe it's time I did.'

'But we'll need an outfit,' Buck Theodore said, still held with an old man's doubt. 'Where'll we get that?'

'From Asa Bingham,' Tracy explained.

'What you aimin' to use for money?'

'Our faces, just our honest faces. Come on, we got things to do!'

CHAPTER EIGHT

In the land office, things were slow. Rufe Wilkens, the agent, had been around for a time in the morning, then had gone off somewhere and had not returned. Now it was a full hour past midday and Mark Kenna, the clerk, had the place to himself. And was bored to death.

For he was weary of Maacama Basin, weary of this sprawling, dusty town of Antelope. Weary also of wagon men and grangers, with the brand of poverty and hardship ground into them and who brought to the office their endless questions and requests, drawn by the dream and lure of

131

free land.

Most were crude and unlettered, scarce able to read or write their own name. Yet, because he himself was one with little resource in character or ability, and had scraped up barely enough education to qualify for his minor job, Kenna felt immensely superior to these fumbling, but deeply earnest men, and viewed them with a thinly concealed contempt.

Truth was, he had not wanted to come to Maacama Basin in the first place. But the Bureau had ordered it so, and because he needed the job, and badly, he was here. But he wished himself far away, back in some big city where things were going on, where people knew how to live and where there were beautiful women and lots of them, who could appreciate a man like Mark Kenna, with his eye for beauty and his taste for clothes and living.

Beautiful women! Hell! One of the very few good-looking ones in this damned place was a granger girl who had been in the office with her father, a man named Vail, as Kenna recalled it, John Vail.

Irked with his thoughts, Kenna built and lit one of his husk cigarettes, then circled from behind the counter and hooked a shoulder point against the post of the open door, there to survey the run of Antelope's main street with a jaundiced eye. People moved up and down and wagons creaked by, churning up the street's acrid dust. Further along, at Asa Bingham's store, three saddle men pulled in and dismounted.

As little use as he had for grangers, Kenna had even less for saddle men. Because you could tell off most grangers, put them in their place. But when you tried that with saddle men you could easy stir up an argument for yourself. But to hell with all grangers and saddle men! He wished he was back in Omaha or Denver or Kansas City.

He thought of the granger girl again, the Vail girl. She'd been pretty, all right, damned pretty. Which reminded him of another good-looking one. Tasker Scott's wife. Now there was a real beauty! He'd never seen her real close up, only from here out to the center of the street a time or two when she had driven by in her flossy buggy with the fine matched team of bays. Haughty, that one was, but sure good-looking in a dark, stormy way.

And she was Tasker Scott's. There was a man who had everything. A big ranch. An office in town. Owned a lot of the town, he did, and held claim to property all over the basin. Yeah, a handsome wife and lots of money. Boss of the whole damn basin, you might say. That was it, Tasker Scott had everything. While he, Mark Kenna, what did he have?

Just a minor, tiresome, unrewarding job. Always subject to orders from other men, with a future that was no future. Only one thing guaranteed a man a future. That was money. And he, Mark Kenna, had neither money or the prospect of some.

Self-pity and envy welled up in him like bitter acid.

Then it was Tasker Scott himself who showed on the far side of the street, to start across, angling for the land office. Sight of him brought the idea which quickened Kenna's pulse and put a touch of color in his drab cheeks. He spun the butt of his half-smoked cigarette into the street, moved back of the counter again and waited there.

Tasker Scott's humor was not good. There had been the argument with Lucy last night, which was the dregs of the ruffling up he had given her the other day in his town office. Woman-like, she'd never admit she had it coming, of course, but would go on using it as a club to make things as miserable for him as she could. And she didn't care what she said, either. Like she had no use or respect for him any more. Things of that sort. Not that she really meant it of course; that, she couldn't afford, when everything was considered. But it sure kept a man upset and made his home uncomfortable.

These were the thoughts Tasker Scott had been living with all morning, and as he now circled the counter to the rear room of the land office, both his manner and his words were brusque.

'Wilkens in?'

Mark Kenna shook his head.

'Where is he?'

'Don't know,' Kenna informed. 'He went out about half past nine this morning. I haven't seen him since.'

Scott scowled his disappointment. 'He comes in, tell him I want to see him. Incidently, any more activity or questions by anybody about the country around Smoky Pass?'

The color in Kenna's face quickened. 'Granger was in about it, yesterday. Man named Vail.'

'What did he want?'

'All he could find out about the area. And to see the map.'

'You show it to him?'

'Sure. He had the right to see it.'

'You've been told different.'

Mark Kenna shrugged. 'Maybe. But not loud enough.'

'And just what do you mean by that?' Scott demanded, his eyes pinching down.

'I mean,' Kenna said, 'that money talks. So far I haven't seen any.'

Scott turned quite still for a moment, staring. Then he spoke with slow emphasis.

'We had an agreement. Wilkens and you

and me. That I'd transfer title to land, plenty of good land, to both of you, once the records were all squared and solid. Right?'

Mark Kenna shrugged again. 'I'm not interested in land, sometime in the future. I'm interested in money, now!'

There, he thought. Now you got it, Scott—clear and simple.

Tasker Scott drew a deep breath and then his words fell, thin and soft.

'And if you don't get the money—'

Kenna hesitated ever so slightly, for there was distinct menace in Scott's question. Yet he knew if he was to gain anything out of this stand he had just taken, he had to go through with it now. He had to stick to his guns. He squared himself.

'I'll just have to tell the grangers and anybody else interested, the whole truth. Which is that the Smoky Pass area is open land for any man's homestead.'

'You wouldn't dare!' Tasker Scott purred.

'Think not? Just try me!'

Instead, Tasker Scott hit him, ramming a savage fist into the side of his face, knocking him down. There was plenty behind the blow and when Scott locked a hand on Kenna's shoulder, hauling him up again, the clerk's eyes were dazed and rolling and his knees rubbery. Scott slammed him against the wall and held him there, slapping him across the face until Kenna's head lolled loosely. After which Scott told him things, and harshly.

'Going to hold me up, eh? Make me pay through the nose? Rawhide money out of me? You miserable bastard! Well, you found out something. I made a deal with you and Wilkens. I intend to keep my part of it, and by God you're going to keep yours. You don't, then I won't just slap you around. I'll twist your damned neck!'

He let go and stepped back. Kenna slithered limply down, half sitting, half lying against the base of the wall. A darkening welt stood out on the side of his face and a trickle of blood leaked from his punished lips. His head sagged.

Tasker Scott stared at him, spat and turned away. He looked in at the back room and finding it empty, returned to the street.

A long minute went by before Mark Kenna found the will and strength to regain his feet. He weaved into the rear room, dropped into a chair and mopped shakily at his lips with the back of his hand. Abruptly an almost febrile fury convulsed him, shaking him as with a chill.

It was something which demanded utterance and Kenna gave way to the need, cursing Tasker Scott blindly and senselessly, with only the office walls to hear. When the scalding words finally ran out, Kenna pushed to his feet and crossed unsteadily to a side

137

table which held an empty glass and a pitcher of tepid, slightly stale water. He lifted the pitcher and drank greedily from it, then slopped at his face and head with the balance of the water until the blood was washed away and only the stain of the bruise and the ache of it remained.

Out in the street, Tasker Scott paused for a little time, held with a cold and wicked anger. Kenna! That slippery, conniving whelp! Trying to bleed him, to push him around, to hold a club over him. Over him, Tasker Scott!

Now, more than ever, did Scott want to see Rufe Wilkens. Though his original purpose in seeking the land agent was now pushed far into the background by the implication of what Kenna had attempted. For how much of this was Kenna's own doing; would he have dared such a rank holdup on his own? Or had he done it with Rufe Wilkens's consent and at his direction?

The more Scott considered the matter, the more likely did this second possibility appear. And just where in hell was Wilkens?

Scott turned into the Trail House, hoping to find his man there. But the place was empty except for a couple of wagon men in desultory argument over some minor matter. Scott called for a double whiskey and put it away, welcoming the fiery bite of the heavy jolt, for it matched his mood.

Back in his own office he tried to put the mood aside and concentrate on some paper work which needed doing. But he had no luck with this, either, as the figures persisted in running together, while the information they carried failed to register. So he was soon on his feet again, lighting up a cigar, then pacing restlessly up and down, as was his way when hag-ridden by frustrating and angry thought.

Meantime, further along the street, having but shortly ridden into town, Lee Tracy, Jack Dhu and Buck Theodore were in Asa Bingham's store, listing their needs for an outfit. Asa Bingham waved a hand.

'Help yourselves. Pay when you're able to. Until then, don't worry about it. Because I won't.'

Jack Dhu headed straight for the gun rack, there laying out three Winchesters, a Colt belt gun for him and another like it for Buck Theodore, and ammunition for all five weapons. At Tracy's questioning glance, he shrugged.

'This morning a couple of bully boys put guns on Buck and me. They meant business. They were ready and willing to shoot if they had to. The point is, that's the kind of deal we're up against, and if we expect to see this thing through and to come out ahead, then we damn well better be ready and willing to burn a little powder.'

139

'You're right, of course,' Tracy agreed reluctantly. 'But I hate to think of matters coming to that pitch.'

'Hell, yes!' said the Texan. 'I do, too. Gunplay is always bad business. But when it's shoved at you, what else you going to do?'

Having thus settled the point, he began cleaning the factory grease from the weapons and Tracy joined Buck at the far end of the store to make a pile of blankets and other essential gear and supplies. Some time later the three of them left for the land office.

When they turned in here, Mark Kenna watched them warily from behind the counter. One side of his face was dark and swollen, and his lips were puffed. He hoped these saddle men weren't out to give him any rough time, because the reaction of his row with Tasker Scott was really at work. His head ached wickedly, his legs were shaky again, and his stomach was rank and burning from the bitterness of spleen.

Tracy gave him the word briefly.

'We're homesteading. We've run our lines, set out corners. Now we want to file. Trot out the necessary papers and records.'

Kenna made no comment until he had spread several official forms on the counter. Then he asked, 'Where are your claims?'

'Right in below Smoky Pass.'

Watching closely, Tracy saw Kenna stiffen

140

slightly, while a gleam lit up his dulled, sick-looking eyes.

'The other day,' Tracy reminded, 'you said that land was already filed on by Tasker Scott. But there is no sign of occupancy or improvement of any kind on it, and the law says there must be both to make the claim valid. So—?'

'I was mistaken in what I told you before,' Kenna said. 'That particular stretch of land is wide open. So your claims will be good, providing you comply with the occupancy and improvement clauses.'

'Which, of course, we'll do,' Tracy said.

Near an hour later, when they were once more back on the street, Jack Dhu made pungent observation.

'That feller looked like he might have run into the south end of a mean horse.'

'For a fact, he must have bumped into something,' Tracy agreed. 'And has changed his tune about the Smoky Pass vicinity. I wonder why?'

'Probably realized he couldn't put a shindy over on us,' suggested the Texan.

'Don't make no difference,' put in Buck Theodore a little wearily. 'We got our land. Now let's get back to it and see can we throw together a decent camp before sundown. I'm going to miss my bunk tonight.'

'We'll have a good camp,' soothed Tracy. 'You two wait for me at the store. I'll be along pretty quick.'

'Where you going?' demanded old Buck.

'There's a man I want to see.'

'Tasker Scott?' Buck guessed shrewdly.

'Yes. And I want to see him alone.'

Buck stared narrowly. 'What you got in your head, boy? You aiming to prove somethin'?'

'Not exactly prove anything. Just to let him know I mean business, and give him a chance to square things without any big trouble.'

'Now there,' declared Buck bluntly, 'you'll be wasting your time and breath. Any man who's gone as far as Scott has along a crooked trail, ain't to be headed back on to a straight one. He's been takin' a long gamble, and was he to back up now, even a little, then he could lose everything. Which he knows. Boy, you won't get nowhere, trying to easy-talk him.'

'Maybe not,' Tracy said soberly. 'But I'm going to try.'

He tramped away and Jack Dhu frowned after him.

'He's level-headed, Tracy is,' mused the Texan softly. 'And he's got his share of salt. So he's not out to easy-talk this Scott hombre because he's afraid of him. There's some other reason behind this.'

'Yeah,' stated Buck, 'and I think I know what it is. I told you how it used to be

142

between Lee and Lucy Garland before she up and married Tasker Scott. Lee thought a powerful lot of that girl. Maybe he still does. What he could be up to is try and head off anything that could hurt Lucy real bad, while seeing to it that we get back at least some of what's ours.'

'Why then,' said Jack Dhu, 'I sure wish him luck. I'm thinking he'll need it. Our little tilt with those two hardcases at the line camp told me all I need to know about them and the man who hired them. You don't get anything back from that breed, Buck, unless you fight for it.'

Tasker Scott was still on his feet, still pacing his office when Lee Tracy turned in at the door. Scott came around quickly, and his face, made loose and working and undisciplined by the thoughts that had been plaguing him, began pulling into a taut, guarded mask.

'You're not welcome here, Tracy. You should know that.'

Tracy shrugged. 'True enough. Yet I'm here.'

'What do you want?'

'A talk, and a show of common sense.'

Scott moved in behind his desk, spread his hands on it and stood leaning slightly forward, as though in challenge.

'You got anything to say, say it! Then get out. I've no time for you.'

143

Eyeing Scott levelly, Tracy faced him across the desk top.

'Good enough. Here it is. For a start, you owe me and Buck Theodore two hundred and eighty-seven head of first grade, white faced cattle.'

'I what?' The words burst out explosively. 'Two hundred and eighty-seven head of cattle? That I owe you and Theodore? You're out of your mind! You got a hell of a nerve bringing that kind of talk into this office.'

'Maybe so,' said Tracy steadily. 'But you had a worse one when you shipped that many head of vented Flat T Herefords from Comanche Junction without going to the trouble of buying them from Buck. I always knew you were in a hurry, Tasker, so much so that you didn't give much of a damn who you stepped on. But to travel that fast and leave yourself so wide open—' Tracy shrugged again.

Tasker Scott's eyes turned as blank and hard as his face. But the high degree of inner tumult showed in the way the muscles at his jaw corners bunched and crawled. And his hands, which had been flat on the desk top, now hooked slightly, the knuckles lifting, the finger tips pulling under, like claws. His words became heavy.

'I don't know what the hell you're talking about.'

'Oh, I think you do,' murmured Tracy. 'The record and the figures are all there. Two hundred and eighty-seven head shipped to Gimball & Reese in Kansas City. So how about it? You got a bill of sale for the cattle? No? Then you owe us that many.'

Scott was silent for a moment, gathering his thoughts. 'I didn't need any bill of sale. The Flat T cattle I shipped became mine when I took over Flat T headquarters and range. Asa Bingham held a mortgage on that ranch. I bought it up and foreclosed when Buck Theodore couldn't meet it. And the cattle went with the range.'

Tracy shook his head. 'Won't do. Won't do at all. Because you didn't foreclose and take over the ranch until after you'd helped yourself to our cattle.'

Scott pressed harder against the desk. 'Would you be calling me a thief?'

'Do you know of a better word?' retorted Tracy. 'What else are you when you steal?'

Scott cursed and made as if to come around the desk. He found himself looking into the cold, blue eye of Tracy's gun.

'Stop right there!' Tracy warned. 'Not that I'd ever be afraid to take you on, Tasker—man to man. For I think I'm tougher than you are; sure of it, in fact. I think maybe you've been living too high and that inside you're a little soft. But just now I got neither the time or the mood to find out.

I came here to lay a few things on the line, and that I'm going to do. Get back behind that desk and sit down!'

A wave of the gun emphasized the words. Scott, face turgid with his anger, did as he was told.

'Better,' Tracy said, putting the gun away. 'Now let's not try and dodge or sidestep. Let's admit the facts. And get this. I'm not wanting to start a war; or do I want any trouble that can be avoided. In fact, I'm really being generous, giving you the chance to return what you took from Buck Theodore and me. You do and we'll call it square. Which is a better deal than you deserve, but one we're willing to go through with.'

Tasker Scott stared at him, unwinking. Then he laughed, short, barking and without mirth.

'You're talking to the wrong man, Tracy. You can't bluff me. Any Flat T cattle I shipped were mine. They were part of the ranch—and you can't prove otherwise.'

'If I can't,' Tracy told him, 'then the calendar is wrong. Because the shipping invoices I looked at carried dates. And I think Asa Bingham can furnish the date he sold the mortgage paper to you; Asa is pretty thorough that way. So, are you going to play it fair and sensible or do I have to go to the whip?'

146

'You heard what I said,' defied Scott. 'You can't bluff me!'

Tracy measured him with another long, intent glance, then nodded.

'So be it. You want it rough. That's the way it will be. Those two hardcases you've had holed up at Flat T headquarters, and who you had run Buck Theodore out of the old line camp—get rid of them, Tasker. Head 'em out of Maacama Basin, or they're quite liable to be delivered to you on a board. They threw the first gun. Jack Dhu and me, we'll throw the last one, if it must be that way. One thing you can be sure of, you're going to pay Buck Theodore and me what you owe us. Incidentally, just to keep the record straight, Buck, Jack Dhu and me, we've just filed homestead claims under Smoky Pass. Fellow in the land office told us there'd been a mistake about that land, that you hadn't filed on it after all, and that it was open to any legitimate claim. We're digging in there. We figure on making our claims stick.'

He moved to the door, paused there. 'Last chance, Tasker. You want to play it fair?'

'Get out!' blurted Scott heavily. 'Get the hell out!'

For some little time after Tracy was gone, Tasker Scott stared at the empty doorway. Out beyond it the afternoon sunshine poured whitely down on the street. Dust, churned

147

up by passing hoof and wheel, scattered and settled, a wisp of it drifting through the doorway to lay a parched scent in the warm air. With it came the sounds of the town, the rap-rap of a hammer and the whine of a saw where some new construction was going on. Boot heels clumped past the open doorway and left behind was the fading growl of men's voices. One carefree soul passing by was whistling cheerfully.

But Tasker Scott neither smelled the dust nor saw the sunshine nor heard any of the voices of the town. He was locked away in a vise of thought and emotion which shut out all else but a baffled fury and a taunting shadow of uncertainty he could neither ignore or rationalize out of being.

What was it Tracy had said about him being in so great a hurry that he'd left himself wide open? And hadn't Lucy said something about going too far, too fast? And could they both be right?

Face again twisted by the pressure of inner tumult, he beat softly on his desk with a clenched fist. Why in hell did Tracy have to return to Maacama Basin? And how could anyone have guessed that he would?

Scott lay far back in his chair, forcing himself to relax. He couldn't afford to panic now. He had to clear his mind of all fog of indecision or doubt or worry. He had to start thinking in a straight line again, to correctly measure future possibilities and arrange how to meet them.

CHAPTER NINE

Morning sunlight was playing at the window of her room when Lucy Scott awoke. Normally the most vigorous of persons, she now lay wan and listless, low in mind and spirit, knowing no normal urge to rise and meet the realities of another day. For she had been late getting to sleep last night and had slept poorly after she did. In fact, for the past several nights she had not slept well, harrassed as she was by the feeling that she was trapped in a web of fact and frustrating circumstance which seemed to offer no avenue of escape.

From the moment when, in his town office, her husband had laid violent hands on her, shaking her as he might have a refractory child, thus stripping her of all dignity and respect, a consuming bitterness had been her full portion. And with it came reluctant, but full and inescapable acceptance of something that had been growing in realization for months; the fact that she was married to a man she did not love, never really had, and now never could. For love presupposed an accompanying respect, and of this she had

149

none at all for Tasker Scott. And very little for herself, for that matter.

She rubbed a hand across eyes that were aching and dry. Never one for tears, she would have welcomed some now if they could have done any good. But they couldn't. Nothing, it seemed, could. For in marrying Tasker Scott she had sorted out the various values of life and made her choice. Now she had to live with the dismal realization that she had made the wrong one. She had placed material values above the more enduring ones, and these were now mocking her.

Never had the ranchhouse been so empty as these past few days. And nights—particularly the nights. Like last night. Tasker Scott had slept in the adjoining room, but she had neither seen nor spoken with him. He had eaten supper with the crew again, then had spent some time in the ranch office. After which he had gone off somewhere not to return until late. It had been midnight when she finally heard him come in and go to bed just beyond that adjoining wall. And she knew that by this time of morning he was long up and gone again.

Well, that was all right, too, for nothing would have been gained by them facing each other; she could know relief over that. Yet the sense of an almost overpowering loneliness was like a weight on her shoulders, along with baffling indecision as to what to do about it.

Never had she realized how much she had leaned on and been swayed by her father in the past. It had always been so easy to let him supply the answers to her most difficult problems. Yet, despite her now forlorn feeling of need for him, she also knew a bite of resentment toward old Hack Garland, because he had influenced her toward Tasker Scott. In short, she was a person who had grown up thoroughly spoiled and selfish, and was now face to face with some of life's more brutal truths and was at a loss how to handle them.

Nagged by her thoughts and unable to any longer find creature comfort by lying in bed, she pushed aside the covers, got up, washed and dressed and worked at her hair with considerable care, for she had long known that this was one of her physical charms and so was ever careful to make the most of it.

She went into the ranchhouse kitchen and stirred up a fire in the stove. Considering what she would have for breakfast she decided that coffee alone would be enough, so set a pot of it on to heat. Waiting for this to turn over, she opened the front door of the house and stepped out on the long, deep porch.

From here was offered a far-reaching view

of the flat, long-running miles of Maacama Basin. On a clear morning such as this it was possible to pick out the glint of sun on Antelope town's distant windows. While away and beyond all of it lifted the misted bulk of the Mingo Hills.

Through the still, warming air, familiar ranch sounds came to her. The muted bawl of a cow. The thin, shrill squeal of quarreling horses in the cavvy corral. The twitter of swallows under the eaves of the big barn. The piping, off-key whistling of the ranch cook as he rattled pans in the cookshack.

A sudden rush of emotion gripped Lucy Scott. She had never known any other home but this ranch. Here she had been born, here she had grown up, and every nook and corner and foot of it was as familiar to her as the palm of her hand. How deeply she loved it all, for it was as vital to her needs as the very blood in her veins.

But was it to become nothing more than an empty mockery?

Now a mist did blur her eyes and it was after she had brushed this away that she saw the rider swing into view past the corrals. There was no mistaking who it was. How many times in older and happier days had she watched the same lean, casually erect figure come jogging up in just this way! Within her a silent voice cried feverish, but soundless welcome.

'Lee! Lee Tracy!'

Tracy had ridden in on the Lazy Dollar with about equal amounts of caution and grimness. Full sight of the ranchhouse brought a flood of memories. Memories of evenings spent on that broad porch with Lucy Garland, and of all the fine dreams he had fashioned there. But also memory of that bitter day when Lucy and Tasker Scott and Hack Garland had stood on that same porch and how they had looked and acted while Hack had given him the word of Lucy's sudden marriage to Tasker Scott.

The place seemed quiet enough. In an open faced shed beyond the ranchhouse stood the shiny buggy Lucy had been driving when he'd seen her in town, so he figured she was home. The next moment he was sure of it as she stepped from the deeper shadow of the porch into the sunshine at the edge of it. When he reined in at the foot of the steps she exclaimed her pleasure.

'Lee! I knew you'd come to me.'

He dismounted and looked at her gravely, knowing a small feeling of irritability. Evidently she still felt she held the old power over him, and just now he wasn't too sure that she didn't. For despite a hint of wanness about her eyes and mouth, the same old sultry, dark, exciting beauty was there. He tried to keep his tone casual as he climbed the steps to her side.

'I came because I had things to tell you, Lucy. Things I'm afraid you won't enjoy listening to.'

She made a small face. 'I'm interested only in talking about you and me, Lee. I was just about to have some coffee. Come and have some with me.'

The living room was big and cool and shadowed. It had its memories, too, Tracy reflected.

Lucy turned abruptly, came close to him, put her hands on his arms and stood staring up at him. She nodded.

'The same man. A little older—but the same man.'

Tracy shook his head, his tone running dry.

'No, Lucy. The older part is right—but not the same man. The Lee Tracy you knew belongs in the past. This is a different one.'

'I don't believe it,' she retorted. 'There was always something safe and steadfast about you, Lee. I was the stinker. And if it's any satisfaction to you, I've paid—plenty!'

'Folks who try to play both ends against the middle generally do, Lucy.' Again he spoke dryly as he tried to move away from her.

But she clung to him and before he could stop her, her arms were about his neck, she had pulled his head down, and her lips were warm and pulsing against his own.

154

For a moment there was a blind confusion of his senses, and then a curious calm ran through him. For there was no sweetness for him here, only a cold distaste. And he knew in this moment that any spell Lucy Scott had once held for him was completely dead. This was not the girl he'd once known love for. This was just another man's wife, a selfish woman whose only sense of values, apparently, was her own personal desires. And the fervor of her kiss left him completely unmoved.

He pulled her arms from about his neck, held her away from him.

'It won't do, Lucy. You're married, remember? You're Mrs Tasker Scott. No, it won't do.'

She stared at him, for a moment almost girlishly appealing. Then she exclaimed with a small fierceness.

'Tasker Scott! Maybe I hate him. Maybe I despise him!'

Tracy nodded. 'Something probably inevitable from the start. But the fact remains—you're still his wife. And to me, just another woman.'

'I don't believe it, Lee. You're not the sort to change.'

'Time changes many things,' he told her steadily. 'Circumstances, too. The old days, and what they once held, are dead, Lucy.'

She studied him intently, almost

yearningly. Then, slowly, a hardness came into her eyes and formed about her lips, thinning them and the words they spoke.

'If they are, then why are you here?'

'I came to have that talk you spoke of when I saw you in town.'

She tossed a dusky head. 'Maybe I'm not interested, now.'

'That would be your right,' he admitted. 'But what I have in mind is pretty important.'

'All right,' she said abruptly. 'I'll listen.'

She led the way into the kitchen, where the coffee had begun to murmur and steam. Many times before had he been in this room and sat at this table. Many times had he talked across it, and argued, too, with Hack Garland—useless arguments with a tough, autocratic, opinionated old-timer who never had been able to shed the harsh, horny-handed ruthlessness that a hard earlier life had ground into him.

Perhaps, Tracy mused, somewhat irrelevantly, the chief reason Hack Garland had always shown him a greater edge of hostility than one of friendship was because he had never stayed with the old fellow in an argument until he had him thoroughly nailed down. There were some like that; you had to whip them at their own game to make them respect you.

With a little start, he realized that while

the image of Hack Garland was easy to recall, that of the Lucy Garland of those earlier days was not. The image of the girl he remembered was so dim now as to be little more than a shadow. It was like trying to recapture a brief glimpse of a swift-passing beauty, or savor again a touch of fragrance born on a vagrant wisp of breeze, poignantly sweet at the moment, but once gone, never to be recalled except in wistful and fading memory.

Watching the real substance of her now as she busied herself pouring coffee, he saw her in a much harder and more practical light. Undeniable beauty was there, dark and sultry, but it meant nothing to him. Very definitely was he able to settle one thing beyond all future doubt. A personality he had once known and held dear, was forever gone into the mists, replaced by another that might easily be classed as a stranger.

Far from any sense of regret, he drew comfort from the realization. It would make much easier the task he had set for himself.

She put a steaming cup in front of him, then took the chair across the table, showing another abrupt change of mood.

'Tasker would be furious if he knew of this.'

'Probably,' Tracy agreed. 'Which is why I made certain he wasn't around before I rode in.'

Her lip curled slightly. 'Still afraid, Lee?'

'No.' His tone turned crisp. 'Not in the least afraid. But I knew I'd get nowhere trying to talk to you if he was around. We had a little session in town yesterday, Tasker and I, and I came away from it feeling it was useless to try and reason with him. Maybe he told you about it?'

She shook her head. 'What was it about—this session?'

'Several things. But mainly cattle.'

'Cattle?'

'That's right. Cattle your husband stole from Buck Theodore and me.'

Tracy made the statement carefully but explicitly, watching closely past the rim of his cup. He saw her shrink slightly, while her glance slid away.

'You knew about the cattle, didn't you, Lucy?'

She evaded the question with a show of defiance.

'Tasker had a right to take over Flat T. There was a mortgage. He bought it up and—'

'I know all about that,' Tracy broke in. 'But he stole the cattle before he ever got hold of the mortgage. If he hadn't taken the cattle first, he wouldn't have been able to foreclose. Because Buck Theodore would have been able to realize enough on the cattle to pay off the claim. For that matter, if

158

Buck hadn't been pushed to the wall by loss of the cattle, he wouldn't have had to borrow any money from Asa Bingham in the first place. No, Lucy, your husband pulled a very smooth piece of banditry.'

'How do you know I wasn't in on it?' Again she was defiant.

'I don't,' Tracy said quietly. 'I prefer to think that you weren't.'

She searched his face with a veiled glance. 'Why don't you make up your mind about me?'

He tipped a shoulder. 'I have. But I still don't want to hurt you, personally. Which happens to be the truth, whether you believe it or not.'

'Assuming what you charge against Tasker is correct, what would you expect me to do about it?'

'Talk to him. Try and persuade him to do the right thing by Buck and me without us having to force the issue. That's it, talk to him.'

Her laugh was a low and twisted thing.

'Why not ask me to sprout wings and fly? It would be easier.'

'Easier?'

'Yes, easier!' she reiterated with bitter emphasis.

She brooded a moment, head bent. Then her head came up and she faced him squarely and he saw clearly the feverish

159

misery in her eyes and read the whole truth behind it.

'Your marriage hasn't worked out very well, has it, Lucy,' he said gently.

Again that twisted, wounded laugh.

'It hasn't worked out at all. So, if you've ever wanted to get even with me for the way I treated you, know that you're more than even, now.'

Abruptly he wanted out, to get away. Further talk was useless, for it was going in the wrong direction. And his feeling was that here he was looking at a woman who had been robbed of everything, particularly her self-respect. He got to his feet and said the only thing he could say, even though it was trite.

'I'm sorry, Lucy.'

'Don't be,' she retorted. 'If you've nothing else for me, I don't want your pity.'

He left the house quickly and she let him go without further word. With him he carried a sense of bleak distaste, thinking how only a brief glimpse at true ugliness was all that was needed to identify it beyond all mistake. And the ranchhouse he had just left was full of the tawdry shadows of marital conflict and unhappiness.

Stepping into his saddle he reined away past the corrals where he underwent the tight-eyed scrutiny of a lounging ranch hand, a narrow faced fellow with a stub of a cigarette pasted in one corner of his mouth. And even when far out in the flats it seemed to Tracy he could still feel the impact of that hostile stare.

*　*　*

In town, Rufe Wilkens and Tasker Scott faced each other across Scott's desk. Tension ran strongly between them. Wilkens spoke with a blunt defiance.

'You want to know where I've been? I'll tell you. I've been taking a real good look at Maacama Basin, at all of it. I've covered a lot of miles. I didn't get back to town until close to midnight. It was a long ride, but worth it.'

'You must have liked what you saw,' remarked Scott sarcastically. The barest flicker of wariness crept into his glance.

'I liked it all right,' Wilkens emphasized. 'I liked it plenty! So we've some readjustments to make, you and me.'

Scott stirred in his chair. 'What kind of readjustments?'

Wilkens shrugged. 'Let's call it a definite transfer of title to proven property, now! Instead of a verbal promise of the same in some indefinite future.'

Quick anger washed through Scott's cheeks.

'You don't trust me, is that it?'

The land agent shrugged again.

'Considerable experience down across the years has left me with little real trust of anybody, even myself. You might say I've become a thoroughly cynical realist.'

'You feel you're in position to swing a club on me?'

'I'm sure of it.' There was smooth mockery in Wilkens's reply.

'So!' rapped Scott harshly. 'Just another damned rat. Same breed as Kenna. Only he tried to gouge me for straight money. Well, I soon convinced him of his mistake!'

'Sure,' drawled Wilkens easily. 'You roughed him up, cuffed him around. Here's a word of caution, Scott. Don't ever try handling me that way. Because in such matters as that, we're not at all of the same makeup, Mark Kenna and me.'

Wilkens dredged about in a vest pocket and came up with the cold stub of a half-smoked stogie. He used three matches and considerable gross smacking of lips before he got the butt lit and drawing to his satisfaction. Then, squinting through the stale, strong smoke, he put the full weight of his glance on Tasker Scott and spoke again.

'You might as well listen to reason. Because if you're playing with any wild ideas, forget 'em! You can't hurt me half as much as I can you.'

'Word to the right quarter in Washington can have you out of a job and facing prosecution within a month,' charged Scott.

Rufe Wilkens leaned back in his chair and drew leisurely on his stogie. A small, sardonic smile pulled at his lips.

'I fail to worry. The possibility is too remote. Serious prosecution is so improbable as to be virtually non-existent. The act is too trivial and the process too ponderous. I know, Scott, I know! As for the job, I never did see it as of any real account, being poorly paid and with damn little future. As a matter of fact, I have for some time been looking for a chance to chuck it and get hold of something where I can really make a stake for myself. And I've decided that right here and now is the time and place.'

Tasker Scott got out a cigar, himself. By the time he had it lit and drawing freely, his features were masked, his eyes shadowed.

'There was some particular stretch that you liked?'

'Yes,' Wilkens said. 'The Flat T layout. With that, and maybe a hundred head of cattle as a starter, I can see where my old age might be quite secure and comfortable.'

Scott's scoffing laugh held no mirth. 'Why not ask me for both legs and my right arm? The answer of course is—no!'

'I expected that,' nodded Wilkens blandly. 'But you haven't considered things real careful. When you do you'll come to my way of thinking.'

'Like hell!' Scott told him flatly. 'And I don't go along with that talk of you hurting me more than I can hurt you, either. So where does that leave you?'

'Right where I was before, in the driver's seat. Let's say the word was spread that all your filed claims were invalid. How long do you think it would be before grangers would be on those particular parcels like a swarm of ants?'

'You'll have plenty of trouble convincing anyone of that,' Scott retorted. 'My reputation with the grangers is sound. I opened this basin to them and they won't—'

'Come down to earth, man, come down to earth!' broke in Wilkens. 'You're not talking to some drifter who doesn't know any better. You're talking to me, Rufe Wilkens, land agent. You encouraged grangers into Maacama Basin for just one reason. To serve your own interests. For most of this basin is government land, which, though you covet it, you knew damn well you couldn't make legitimate claim to and make it stick. Even you didn't have quite the gall necessary to attempt that. But you knew how you could get title to it another way. That was to bring grangers in here to file and prove up on homesteads.'

Wilkens, a swarthy, stocky man, coarse in feature, manner and word, pushed to his feet and took a turn about the office.

'Yeah, Scott,' he went on, 'that's how you figured. Because you knew that not one out of five of the grangers, even after they'd proven up and got clear title would settle permanent. Because they're a breed apart. They're grangers because they like to be grangers. They drift because they like to drift. And they never do get shut of the idea that just over the next hill or around the next turn of the trail lies the promised land, much greener and fatter than the one they're on.

'So pretty soon they move on again, and somebody with a little ready money can pick up land titles right and left for a small fraction of what the property is really worth. And who in Maacama Basin would be that somebody? None other than Mister Tasker Scott.'

While he spoke, Wilkens's soggy cheroot butt went out, and when another flaring match failed to bring it alive he threw it out of the open door into the street. He came around and faced Scott.

'And what happens to those who really make a try at sticking? Well, after a little time their troubles begin. The big fellow in the basin, who would be you, Scott, starts putting the pressure on a little fellow here, another poor devil yonder, and being grangers at heart, they begin figuring that the prize isn't worth the game. So they say, "To hell with it!" load the women and kids into their wagon, accept a few dollars for their homestead title and head out once more. So, pretty soon, who owns Maacama Basin from end to end? Up pops that same old devil, Mister Scott. And then, by and by, the railroad comes in. Land values soar. And who has land, lots of land to sell? How do you do, Mister Scott!'

'You spread that kind of word about me and you admit your own complicity,' Scott said, a trifle heavily. 'You drag me down, you go down with me.'

'Don't you ever think it,' taunted Wilkens. 'Right now, so far as the grangers know, I'm the government in this basin. I'm Uncle Sam! And who do you think they will believe if I tell them you falsified your claims, that you'd been found out and the claims denied, with the records adjusted accordingly? That's right—me!'

Scott peered at the tip of his cigar, flicked the ash from it and slowly cleared his throat.

'I can still see to it that the word reaches Washington about how faithful a servant you turned out to be.'

Wilkens scoffed. 'Washington! How far is it from here? A long way, Scott—just a hell of a long way. And what are they going to believe back there? Information from me on an official form, or a crank letter from you? Hell, man, they get hundreds of such a year; somebody is always taking pen in hand to bellyache to the government about something. Even should you manage to stir up an investigation serious enough to amount to anything, by the time it got in operation I'd have all my records in perfect shape and you'd be the fair-haired boy who took the licking. For remember, you're the thief, not me. So think it over good! After all, you already own one ranch, the Lazy Dollar. Why shouldn't I own one, the Flat T?'

'And you'd call me a thief!' said Scott thickly.

Wilkens laughed. 'Well, aren't you? Me, I'm just an honest opportunist.'

Saying which, he moved out into the street.

Scott's glance did not follow him. Instead, it fixed broodingly on the far wall of the office. So this was how the game was to be played, eh? First Stump Yole and High Bob Caldwell trying to rawhide extra money from him. Then Mark Kenna trying some of the same. Now Rufe Wilkens had come up with his wild demand. It had been simple enough to answer Yole and Caldwell and Kenna. Would it be that simple with Wilkens?

In the office, day's warmth thickened. Over against the window a blue-bottle fly set up an insistent buzzing and made small thumping sounds against the glass.

For a full half hour Scott sat without movement, deep in bitter thought. At the end of that time he had reached convincement on three things. The first was that a man could buy only so much loyalty and service. The second was that once a man bent, he was that much closer to being completely broken. And finally, should he accede even in the slightest to the demands that had been thrown at him, then most certainly could he expect more of the same from the same sources. Wolves, he reflected bleakly, were never satisfied.

One way or another, decision had to be reached. Either he drew back and sacrificed all hope of attaining what he had planned and worked toward, or he went ahead, using whatever means necessary to attain his goal. And because he was a greater wolf than any, and did not have it in him to give up any portion of what he had already taken and all he had set out to take, he decided on the second course, regardless of the risk or scantiness of the claim.

Once this was settled, he felt better. Uncertainty, indecision—these, along with weakness in any degree, could confuse a man, and destroy him and all his works.

From a desk drawer he took a snub nosed six-shooter of heavy caliber. He flipped back the loading gate, spun the cylinder to make certain the weapon was fully loaded. Assured of this, he dropped the gun into his coat pocket. He left the office and went down along the street to the livery barn. Five minutes later he rode out of town.

From the door of the land office, Rufe Wilkens watched him go, then turned on Mark Kenna a little savagely.

'I could wring your God-damned neck for the play you made at Scott. I told you to let me handle him. I wanted more time on it. But after the stupid break you made, I had to go after him right away.'

'What difference does it make, now or later?' Kenna argued sulkily.

'It makes a hell of a difference!' Wilkens told him roughly. 'I wanted this fellow Tracy to work on him a little more. Then, with Scott calling for more help, our bargaining hand would have been stronger. But you had to spoil that. You showed him some of our cards, so I had to show him the rest. You speak out of turn again, and it won't be Scott who'll slap you around. It'll be me! And I'll do a more complete job than Scott did.'

CHAPTER TEN

Firelight tapered up redly in early night's gentle dark. Buck Theodore crouched in its radiance, nursing a cup of coffee and staring into the flames. Across from him Lee Tracy hunkered, feeding his thoughts with a cigarette. At the very edge of the glow, half in light, half in shadow, an effect which seemed to rob him of substance, Jack Dhu lounged at ease, propped on an elbow.

Old Buck took another sip of coffee and slowly spoke.

'It won't do, boy. Layin' out here this way won't get us nowhere. Sure we got a fair camp. And grub and blankets. But one of these days it'll be winter again and we'll need a roof over our heads. Where we goin' to get it? We can't stay on Asa Bingham's back forever, either. So if you're dead set on havin' a real try at bustin' Tasker Scott, then you'll have to hit him harder and from a different angle than any you've tried so far. This way he can wait us out until hell freezes.'

Listening, Jack Dhu stirred.

'Gospel, there. You aim to really knock down this feller Scott, you got to go after him and stay after him.'

Tracy had a slow, final drag on his cigarette and flipped the butt into the fire.

'We had to light somewhere. It was a move in the game. There'll be more.'

Buck Theodore swung his gaunt shoulders restlessly, made as if to speak again, thought better of it and resumed his brooding contemplation of the flames. Jack Dhu retreated with him into silence.

This lank, cold-jawed Texan, this Jack

Dhu, had been a lone wolf all his life, drifting from one job to another across a wide spread of country. It had been a hard life, many times barely within the law. The loneliness and necessary self-sufficiency of it had made him hard-shelled, wary and aloof, and he had long counted the gun at his hip his only real friend. But here, in Lee Tracy and Buck Theodore he had found two men he could both like and trust, and in their company knew a contentment he'd never had before.

Lee Tracy spoke again.

'Yes, there'll be more moves. All necessary to get back what Tasker Scott took from us. But I don't want to take the gloves completely off unless there's no other way out. I don't give a thin damn about Scott's hide. But there are others who could be hurt. And I don't like that.'

Buck Theodore bobbed his head up and down, as though a previous conclusion was now confirmed.

'She never showed that kind of concern for you, boy. I thought all feelin' in that direction had been knocked plumb out of you?'

'It has been,' said Tracy quietly. 'Yet, she's a woman, and I never was worth a damn, fighting such. And there are others I'm concerned about. You.'

'I told you to forget about me,' Buck growled. 'If you aim to tie into Scott, go

171

ahead—tie into him! Do what you have to do.'

'In good time, Buck, in good time.'

Tracy got to his feet and moved off into the darkness.

Waiting until certain Tracy was out of hearing, Buck rumbled irritably.

'Just plain too damn decent for his own good, that feller. Pawin' the ground to get at Scott, but holdin' back because of Lucy. And after the way she treated him! Worryin' about me, too. Wish he'd realize I don't count no more. I've had my life, with his all ahead of him. I got a notion to run down Tasker Scott, corner him and empty a gun into him. That'd answer a lot of questions.'

'In one way, yes,' agreed Jack Dhu, 'but in another, no. Even should you get away with it, it wouldn't clear things from Lee's angle. Doing another man's fighting for him never really squares things for him. Should a tough bronc throw you, it's no satisfaction seein' it rode by somebody else. You want to live with yourself again, you got to top that bronc yourself and make it stick. This feller Scott threw Lee and threw him good. Left him with a lot of inside bruises. And those bruises will never heal complete unless Lee himself deals it all back to Scott.'

'Mebbe you're right,' scowled Buck. 'But how's he going to take care of Scott without hurtin' Lucy? Which is what he's shyin' away from.'

Retrospect held Jack Dhu silent for a time before he made murmured answer.

'I can understand why. It's not easy to throw away memories that once were good. It's Lee's problem and he'll figure it out. Just give him time.'

'Yeah, time,' grunted Buck dourly. 'But that could mean time for Scott, now that he knows Lee is after him, to get in another surprise bite like runnin' us out of the line camp. And where's the sense to that?'

'There isn't any,' Jack Dhu admitted succinctly. 'But it's the chance we have to take.'

Some quarter mile north and closer to the river than the camp Lee Tracy and his two companions had set up, John Vail's fire burned. Now that he had decided to stay, and, if necessary, fight for his homestead claim, Vail had begun his improvement work. He had laid out and leveled the spot where his cabin would stand. He had hitched his heavy wagon team to his plow and traced the boundaries of his land with a double furrow. Now, resting from the labor of the day, he smoked his pipe beside the fire, a solid, sturdy man with deeply weathered features.

Secure in their beds beneath the weathered canvas top of the big wagon, the two younger children lifted a sleepy murmur

173

as they said goodnight to their mother. In the firelight across from her father, Kip Vail was finishing up washing the supper dishes. It was just such a night as a thousand others John Vail had known—frugal, simple and holding only the bare fringe of comfort. Yet now particularly satisfying because of a decision arrived at and a work begun.

Done with the dishes, Kip set the wash pan to fully drain and spread her towel by the fire to dry. John Vail looked up at this slim, capable daughter of his with pride and a deep affection and pondered her future with some uneasiness. For he had no illusions of the kind of life his family had had to live; drifting, ever drifting, their only home a wagon. And while now determined to set his roots into this piece of land and make a real try at some kind of permanence, there lay, in the worn, faithful, uncomplaining patience of his wife an accusing reminder of how long he had waited to make this decision.

Was more of the same ahead of Kip? Married to another wagon man and pursuing an aimless dream down across the best years of her life, a dream that would grow ever more gray and elusive while the young and good and eager years ran out into the old and tired ones?

Stung by his thoughts, John Vail stirred restlessly. For he had been guilty of following just a vague dream and so now had no more in the way of possessions to offer his family than what stood about him. That canvas-topped wagon yonder with its scanty, humble contents, and that slow, patient team of horses munching wild hay over there in the dark. A plow. A few other miscellaneous tools. What else?

The restlessness in him became a small edge of panic and he spoke with sudden huskiness.

'I'm sorry, Kip.'

She threw him a quick, startled glance.

'Sorry! What for, Father?'

'For waiting so long before beginning a real home for your mother and you and the young ones. It comes to me that I have not measured up very well.'

Kip was swiftly around the fire to lay an arm across his shoulders.

'There'll be no more of that kind of talk. You've been the best of fathers.'

Vail shook his head. 'I've given you so little—and have so little to offer now.'

'Not so,' insisted Kip. 'You've given us all that really counts; each other and the love that holds us together. The rest doesn't matter.'

She leaned and brushed her cheek against his weathered one. Then straightened and turned at the sound of a step in the outer dark. When she saw who it was moving up to the fire, a quick, welcoming smile framed her lips.

Lee Tracy touched his hat. 'Evening, folks. Seeing as we're neighbors I thought I'd drop by and say howdy.'

John Vail stared. 'Neighbors?'

'That's it. Buck Theodore, Jack Dhu and me—we've homesteaded down river a bit.'

'Well, now!' exclaimed Vail. 'Shows you mean what you preach.'

'To some extent,' Tracy nodded. 'It may stir up some action by Tasker Scott which could reach to you. If that happens, we'll take the fight off your hands.'

'No need of it,' Vail said gruffly. 'I can care for me and mine.'

'I'm sure of it,' Tracy paused before adding, 'providing Scott doesn't get too rough.'

Vail's glance sharpened. 'You make of the man an out-and-out renegade, don't you? I admit he may be a promoter with more greed in him than principle. But I find it hard to believe he'd go beyond that.'

'Tasker Scott will go to any extreme to get what he wants.' Tracy put deliberate emphasis into the words. 'I have positive proof for one thing, that the man is a bare-faced cattle thief.'

'Sounds like a strong grudge between you and Scott,' Vail observed.

'Yes,' Tracy admitted. 'An old grudge.'

176

'What over?'

Tracy hesitated, then shrugged. 'Part that I just told you. He stole close to three hundred head of good white-faced cattle from Buck Theodore and me.'

'Man who'll do that is capable of most anything,' Vail said.

'Anything!' said Tracy. 'So don't trust him at all.'

Kip Vail, who had listened carefully, now stepped past Tracy, caught up an empty water bucket and started for the river. Tracy dropped quickly in beside her, took the bucket from her hand.

'Let me.'

Watching them fade out into the dark, John Vail opened his mouth to call his daughter back, but before he could get the words out, another, and restraining hand dropped on his shoulder. The hand of his wife. She had come quietly down from the wagon. Now she spoke softly.

'Let be, John. It is Kip's right to know someone besides just her family. She is no longer a child.'

'But this fellow Tracy—'

'Is a good man. Nothing else matters.'

In the shelter of the dark, Kip Vail moved lightly along with Lee Tracy, faintly smiling with the age-old wisdom of her sex. Presently she spoke.

'There is more behind your quarrel with

177

Tasker Scott than just loss of cattle. A woman, perhaps?'

Tracy did not answer right away. Then, presently:

'Yes. How did you guess?'

'That kind of a guess is an easy one to make. Was she worth it?'

Tracy considered. 'I thought so at the time,' he said carefully.

'But no longer?'

'No, no longer.'

'Then why not drop the grudge?'

'There's the stolen cattle,' Tracy reminded. 'And the range and a ranch headquarters. Also the measure and value of a man's pride. For these things he must stand his ground and fight. Else he's a whipped dog all the rest of his life.'

Before them the alder and willow growth of the river lifted in blackest shadow, letting through only in part some hint of the vague and distant silver of the stars. Night air, cool and moist, seemed to flow with the water that whispered between the banks. A narrow spread of gravel crunched under Tracy's boots as he leaned and filled the water bucket and lifted it dripping from the depths.

Beside him, Kip Vail stood silent, caught up by the night's wide spell. Abruptly she threw another question.

'This woman, was she pretty?'

'Was and is,' Tracy answered briefly.

'I wonder if I have ever seen her?'

'That I wouldn't know. She is now Tasker Scott's wife.' Tracy put down the bucket of water, brought out his smoking, fashioning a cigarette by feel alone. He scratched a match alight, nursed it in his cupped hands, then lifted it, and as he bent his head to meet it, the match's faint flare briefly highlighted the grave set of his features.

'The day we arrived in Maacama Basin,' Kip Vail said slowly, 'I saw a woman in town. She was no granger woman. She was in a shining buggy, driving a spanking team. She was dark and—and beautiful, I thought.'

'That would be her,' Tracy said. 'Lucy Scott. At one time Lucy Garland.'

Again a silence fell and again it was Kip Vail who broke it.

'I think if I knew her, I would dislike her very much.'

Tracy was startled, not only by the words but by the hint of intensity behind them.

'Why do you say that?' he asked.

The answer came simply. 'I don't like dishonest people.'

Tracy considered this for a moment. 'Does it necessarily mean a woman is dishonest just because she marries the man of her choice?'

Kip tossed her head. 'You're covering up, making it sound too simple. If she didn't treat you fairly, she was dishonest.'

179

'How do you know she didn't?'

'I know,' Kip declared. 'If she'd treated you fair it wouldn't rankle.'

Tracy took a deep drag on his cigarette, spun the butt away. It fell in a small, sparkling arc that quenched in the sliding river water with a tiny hiss. Tracy looked at the girl beside him. A beam of starlight's silver filtered palely through the alders, touching her. Her face was upturned and she seemed to be studying him.

'You,' he observed, 'are a shrewd person, Kip Vail. And pretty enough in your own right.'

'Careful,' she warned, softly laughing. 'Else you'll be turning my head.'

'I wonder?' he murmured.

On swift impulse he bent and kissed her, and the contact left them both stirred and breathless and enormously aware of each other. Now it was Tracy who first found voice.

'I won't say I'm sorry. If I did it would make that meaningless. And it wasn't meant to be.'

'I think,' said Kip quickly, 'we'd better get back to camp.'

She moved away. Tracy picked up the bucket of water and followed. Nearing the fire she slowed her pace so he could come even with her. Again she was softly laughing.

'I think I invited that,' she said. 'And I'm

glad it wasn't without meaning. After all, you never were properly rewarded for what you did for me the first night you saw me.'

'So-o!' Tracy drawled, gently chiding. 'Did somebody mention something about honesty?'

'They did,' Kip affirmed. 'And if that was for dragging me out from under the hoofs of a bunch of water-crazy horses—this—is for itself!'

Swift and light she was on tiptoe and again her lips were on his. Then she was away and gone once more and before Tracy could think up further words, they were both within the radiance of John Vail's fire.

From beneath shaggy brows the granger gave them a brief scrutiny, then returned his gaze to the flames. Beside him, Rachel Vail, with a more searching and understanding glance, marked the shine in her daughter's eyes and the touch of quickened color in flushed cheeks and she smiled wisely to herself.

*   *   *

Tasker Scott made a day of it in the saddle. It had been some time since he had ridden Maacama Basin to any extent, particularly the upper end of it, what with the press of his affairs in and closer around town. Now he was out to sound the general sentiment of

181

the grangers and to test their cohesiveness if any. To this end he stopped at a considerable number of camps and made genial, but carefully calculated conversation. What he discovered confirmed an opinion he'd long had, which was that the average man was mainly concerned for himself and his own, first, last and all the time.

In fact, he discovered a number of squabbles going on among grangers over claims and boundaries, and before the day was done it was increasingly plain that nothing short of the threat of a forced mass exodus from the basin would weld the grangers into a force solid enough to be really reckoned with. Certainly the ousting of a few here and there was not going to overly concern those who were left alone. Once certain of this fact, Scott moved to act.

Late in the day he stopped at the old Flat T headquarters and held a short council with Stump Yole and High Bob Caldwell.

'You want more money,' he said. 'Very well, you'll get it when you earn it. But you got to earn it.'

'How?' grunted Stump Yole.

'By clearing out the granger camps under Smoky Pass. Make them understand that land has already been filed on and they'll have to locate somewhere else in the basin.'

'How much?' Greed filled the squint of Stump Yole's eyes.

Anger lifted in Tasker Scott. Basically, he thoroughly despised these two, this Stump Yole and High Bob Caldwell. Nothing would have suited him better than to take a whip to them like he might to a pair of animals. Some day, he promised himself, and with luck, he would. But just now they were of value to him.

'Fifty dollars,' he said. 'Twenty-five apiece.'

'When?'

'When the job is done, of course.'

'Sometime tomorrow,' Stump Yole said, 'we'll see you in town and collect.'

Riding homeward through the sundown shadows, irritation made Scott restless in the saddle. For it galled him to have to bargain with such as Stump Yole and High Bob Caldwell, while knowing that more of the same was a virtual certainty. However, he told himself, before this game was done it would be his turn, and then he'd take full value for everything gouged from him now.

As usual, at Lazy Dollar, Lonnie Raikes came out of the dusk to take over Scott's mount. He offered greeting in his soft drawl.

'Evenin', Mister Scott.' He paused briefly, then added, 'Missis Scott had company today.'

Scott had stepped from his saddle and was about to head for the ranchhouse. But behind this statement lay a shadowy

183

intonation which brought him sharply around.

'Yes?' The word ended on a rising note.

'Riding man,' murmured Lonnie. 'Missis Scott was on the porch when he showed. She called him Lee.'

Scott stood high and still, held so by a surge of sudden and wild anger. It was all he could do to keep from smashing his fist into Lonnie's face. For it seemed he'd just listened to an announcement that held a thin note of derision, of mockery. Yet, in all fairness, Scott knew this was not so, for if there was one person in whom he felt he could repose complete trust, it was this soft-spoken cowboy. Even though he knew that Lonnie possessed all the coldly savage instincts of a marauding panther.

Scott fought back his anger, waiting until he could keep his voice steady.

'He stay long?'

'Half an hour, maybe,' Lonnie guessed. 'They went inside.'

Scott turned and stared rigidly at the ranchhouse. A lamp, just lighted, bloomed its yellow glow at the kitchen window. As he watched, he saw the head and shoulders of his wife limned between light and window. He drew a deep breath.

'All right, Lonnie,' he said. 'Thanks.'

Lucy Scott was stirring up the fire in the kitchen stove when her husband came in.

From beneath its bowl-shaped, stained glass shade, the lamp spread its greatest light across the table top, so as he stood in half shadow, Tasker Scott's expression was indistinct. But the impact of his unspoken anger reached across the room.

Lucy Scott faced him, saying nothing, waiting him out, wondering a little until his words came.

'You had company today.' It was a flat statement, not a question.

'Company?'

'Tracy.'

'Oh, that.' She shrugged.

'You had him inside.' Again it was a statement.

'For a cup of coffee. A common courtesy.' She flared a little. 'Did the so-gentle, mealy-mouthed Lonnie Raikes try and make more of it? I've had about enough of that fellow hanging around headquarters spying on me. One of these days I'll quit playing the fine lady and turn all daughter of tough old Hack Garland. And I'll run Mister Raikes off the place with a gun!'

'Lonnie's all right,' Scott said thinly. 'I can trust him.'

'But not me, is that it?' Lucy tossed her head. 'Yes, Lee Tracy was here today.'

'What did he want?'

'No part of me, if that's what's troubling you. A fact he made quite plain. If you must know, he came to try and talk sense to both of us.'

'Talk sense!' Scott's eyes widened, then pinched down again. 'What do you mean, talk sense?'

'That we do right by him and Buck Theodore. Oh, he made it plain that he intended to get back everything taken from them, but he hoped this could be done without any real deep trouble. He said he'd already tried to convince you, but without any luck. He suggested I try.'

Tasker Scott laughed harshly. 'The man's a fool. What did you tell him?'

'That I had less chance than he did.'

'You told him right,' ground out Scott. 'There was nothing else?'

Momentarily she mocked him. 'What else could there be? He has no more use for me than he has for you—and who can blame him?' Now her shoulders sagged and she stared straight ahead, pressing her hands against the sides of her face, framing it. 'I think we should do as he asks, Tasker.'

'You'd side with him?'

Lucy shook her head slowly. 'No, it isn't quite like that. But to do the right thing for a change—so there'll be no need of—of—' A little shiver went through her. 'I'm afraid,' she admitted her voice dropping to little more than a whisper. 'Yes, afraid!'

Tasker Scott had seen this sultry wife of

his in many moods, but never one quite like this, and it held him for a moment in uncertainty. Then he jeered.

'It hardly becomes you to admit you're afraid. What of?'

'Nothing, for myself. For you, many things.'

Now he did scoff. 'Concern for me at this stage of the game isn't exactly convincing, my dear.'

She observed him with a steady gravity. 'It's not a bit of use, is it?' she said finally.

'I don't know quite what you're driving at,' he answered bluntly. 'But whatever it is, the answer is no! Like there'll be no more of Lee Tracy visiting you. Lonnie Raikes will have orders to see to that.'

With this final statement, Tasker Scott turned and left, and once more went away through the early dark to have his supper in the cookshack.

CHAPTER ELEVEN

Lee Tracy was early astir. Along the eastern rim of the world, dawn's first thin light was beginning to show, graying the higher slopes of the Mingo Hills. Riverwards it was still all dark shadow and out of these curdled shades the river lifted its chill breath and the wet splashing of its being. Tracy put together a fire and hovered over the frugal beginnings of flame, hands spread to the first touch of warmth.

Restlessness was in him, along with a decision arrived at while he lay long awake last night. He had thought of what Buck Theodore and Jack Dhu had said about moving ahead, of pressing the issue if an issue there must be, and of taking the play away from Tasker Scott. Also he'd thought of Kip Vail, and of the full meaning the touch of her lips had conveyed to him. Meaning of the future, wide and shining. But a future which held nothing unless certain things were taken care of, unless stolen property or its equivalent was recovered and injustice righted. Yes, things to do, for time was fleeting and a man's good years could not be recalled, once he let them get away from him.

Lucy Scott? A shadow of the past, no more. He owed her nothing, not even a lasting memory. If he did, well, he'd pay that by giving her and Tasker their chance to square matters peacefully, a touch of generosity still to be tested. Today he'd get the final answer to that.

Jack Dhu crawled out of his blankets, pulled on his boots and joined Tracy at the fire, taciturn and voiceless as he twisted up the day's first cigarette. Then Buck

188

Theodore joined them, sour and hunched with an old man's early morning grumpiness.

Tracy washed up and cooked breakfast. Hot food and scalding coffee mellowed them and Jack Dhu asked:

'What's it for today?'

'Town,' Tracy said briefly. 'And a final answer from Tasker Scott, one way or another.'

Buck Theodore ceased a somewhat noisy sipping at his coffee and looked up, growling.

'Only answer you'll ever get from him on anything is—no! When you going to get that through your head, boy?'

'I saw Lucy yesterday,' Tracy said. 'I told her what Tasker was going to have to return to us; cattle, our range and our old headquarters. I told her that one way or another, it was what had to be, and for her to try and convince Tasker of the fact. She's had time now to talk to him. I'm finding out if it did any good.'

'It won't,' insisted Buck. 'I can tell you that right now.'

'You're probably right,' Tracy admitted soberly. 'But it is the way I have to handle matters.'

'And when Tasker says "No!"—then what'll you do?'

'I take back what is ours, regardless.'

'A large chore, boy.'

189

Tracy shrugged, spun up a smoke, held a twig in the fire until it flamed, then lit his cigarette.

'Before you get anything away from Tasker Scott now you'll have to kill him,' went on old Buck sagely.

'That may be,' agreed Tracy steadily. 'If so, that's how it will be.'

Buck stared. 'Ain't like you, boy. You never shaped up as a gun-hand.'

'I'm not.' Tracy straightened. 'A man just does what he has to do.'

Jack Dhu got to his feet also. 'This time, you'll want me along.'

Tracy nodded. 'This time, I will. Buck, you mind camp.'

Buck watched them go, rumbling his worry in this throat. The odds, he told himself, were heavy, as they had been from the first. Tasker Scott was organized and dug in. He had such as Stump Yole and High Bob Caldwell, ready and willing to do his bidding—men without conscience and practiced in violence. An old man's fears gripped Buck Theodore and shook him badly.

A sap pocket in a piece of firewood snapped spitefully and a coal was blown clear. Buck quenched this with the dregs of his coffee cup. He put his hands on his hips and pushed up painfully, fighting off morning's stiffness, his face grim under the press of his thoughts.

Up river at the Vail camp breakfast was just getting under way. Rachel Vail and her husband were at the fire and Kip, who had been helping the two children dress, now came along with them from the wagon. There was a tin basin and a bucket of hot water and with great puffings and splashings the youngsters made their quick and scanty morning ablutions, after which Kip began braiding up her small sister's pigtails.

John Vail had greeted this new day with unaccustomed cheer. What with the sound and final decision he'd made for the future, it seemed as if a new vigor had vitalized the air and the stimulation of it all made him eager to get at the real building of a home for his family.

It was Kip who noted the approach of the two riders, and she dropped a single warning word.

'Father!'

John Vail came around, following her nod of direction. The riders had crossed the river a little higher up and were moving in at a driving jog. One of them sat high and narrow and angular in his saddle, while the other, burly and thickset, had legs so short they made him ride with stirrups wide from the horse's sides. Both of them carried belt guns.

As they came closer, John Vail knew a stomach-tightening surge of alarm. So many times along the back trail it had been just such looking men as these who had ridden in on his camps with the same old hated order.

Move along, granger! You're not wanted here!

They came on so purposefully it seemed they might ride right through the fire and John Vail stepped out to meet them. The flanks and legs of their horses were still wet from the river crossing and the burly rider did not stop his mount until it was so close that a restlessly stamped hoof spattered moisture on Vail.

The granger looked up at a face broad and heavy and scarred, with gross lips and little, cruel eyes that swept the camp with a brutal arrogance which momentarily ignored Vail while it insulted his womenfolk. Off to one side, the lanky rider's look and attitude was no better, and Vail knew that here was definite trouble but he stood his ground.

'Something you want?' he demanded.

Now the burly one eyed him directly and spoke in a voice as heavy and brutal as the looks behind it.

'You're on another man's land. Pack your gear and get out!'

Here it was again. The old, old story. *Move along, granger!*

Revolt rose in John Vail.

'No!' he said flatly. 'I'm not on another man's land. I'm on my own claim, filed on

192

and lawfully recorded in the land office. I've ploughed my boundaries, set the spot for my home. Here I stay!'

Stump Yole rested a forearm on his saddle horn, leaned forward to give emphasis to his look and words.

'Granger, I told you to load your gear and move! Don't make me argue the point, because I lose my temper quick when I have to argue!'

By the fire, her sure child's instinct identifying danger, John Vail's little daughter began to whimper and caught at her mother's skirts. John Vail heard the sound and anger blazed in him, hot and righteous.

'No!' he challenged again. 'This is my land. I will not leave it!'

Stump Yole reined his horse sharply, dug in the spurs. Grunting its protest under the rowel punishment, the animal half whirled, then lunged ahead, driving a shoulder in John Vail, knocking him back and almost down. But he recovered and caught at Stump Yole, grabbing him by the belt, then setting back in an attempt to haul him from the saddle.

He came close to succeeding in this, and had Yole leaning wide and near off balance. Then Yole drew his gun and smashed out savagely with it. The heavy barrel of the weapon thudded on John Vail's bared head. His grip on Yole's belt slacked and he fell away limply, to lie still and huddled on the ground.

Stump Yole fought for his balance, recovered it, and, cursing wickedly, brought his horse rearing about as if to send it trampling over John Vail's prone figure. But now it was Kip he had to face. She had darted between him and her father and stood there, face pale, eyes blazing her scorn and contempt.

'Go ahead!' she taunted. 'Hit me. Ride over me. You filthy coward!'

For a moment it showed in Stump Yole's expression that he was tempted to do just that. Then he settled back in his saddle and swung his horse to one side.

'For a granger brat you got spunk,' he admitted. His gross glance ran over her. 'Pretty, too,' he leered. 'Almost too pretty for a granger.'

Now Rachel Vail ran to her husband and dropped down beside him, lifting his battered head and cradling it on one knee. Dabbing at the seep of blood showing in his grizzled hair, she satisfied herself he was alive and already showing a return to consciousness. Then she turned her scorn on Stump Yole and High Bob Caldwell, and it was the more punishing because of its quietness.

'If you're quite through,you can get out and leave us alone. Or do you bully women and children, too? What kind of men are you, anyway? Or are you men at all?'

There were tears in her eyes and her hands were very gentle as she caressed her husband's head and her glance held something that not even Stump Yole's thick rind of stupid brutality was impervious to.

'He asked for it,' blurted Yole defensively. 'He wanted to argue. Anyhow, now you know. I meant it when I said to clear out. See that you do.'

Reining away, he got back some of his bullying self-assurance and paused for a final threat.

'Bob and me, we'll be comin' by this way later on. Don't be here when we do. Else your man will get worse than a gun-whipping.'

They went along then, down river.

Now the small boy and the little girl fled to their mother's side, whimpering their concern for their father. Rachel Vail soothed them.

'Now, now, you must be braver than that. Your father will be all right. Kip, some hot water and towels.'

Ten minutes later John Vail was sitting up, holding a steaming compress to his head. He spoke tightly.

'We're not giving up, Rachel; we're not moving on. If they do come back, I'll be waiting for them with my old Sharp's buffalo gun. No, I won't be driven out!'

Down river, in the first full flare of sunrise, Buck Theodore freshed his fire and put on a bucket of water to heat for the chore of washing out a spare shirt and some socks. He plodded down to the river, searched out an armful of dry firewood drift and carried this back to camp just in time to see Stump Yole and High Bob Caldwell riding in.

He put down his load of firewood and speculated for a moment on the purpose of these two. After which he crossed to his blankets, took his holstered gun from under one corner of them and finished buckling the weapon at his gaunt old hip as Yole and High Bob hauled up at the edge of camp.

Stump Yole eyed him carefully. 'What's the gun for?'

'Maybe I need the weight to keep me balanced,' Buck told him dryly.

'Weight of a gun has tipped more than one man on his face—and for good,' remarked Yole significantly. He glanced around. 'The rest who belong in this camp—where are they?'

Buck shrugged. 'Around.'

High Bob Caldwell had been reading sign. Such as Buck's horse, picketed yonder. And Buck's saddle beside his blankets. But though there were two other spreads of blankets there were no more horses or saddles in evidence.

'Not too close around,' observed High Bob thinly. 'They're off somewhere.'

'Just so,' agreed Stump. 'Old man,' he told Buck Theodore, 'you're ridin', too. Hauling out of here. Because you're on another man's land.'

Buck scoffed. 'Tell that to the land office and see what answer you get. And tell Tasker Scott such a bluff ain't worth a damn.'

'Bluff?' Stump Yole stared. 'Old man, you know better than that. Bob and me, we never bluff. We don't like to argue, either. Stirs us up. And gettin' stirred up makes us mad. After that—' Heavy shoulders gave a significant shrug. 'Move out! Bob and me are stayin' right here to see that you do.'

Buck shook his head. 'Not today or any other. The moving out to be done, you'll do!'

High Bob Caldwell began edging his horse to one side. He stopped this abruptly as Buck Theodore lashed out with harsh and brittle words.

'Not that way! Down river. You can start now!'

They measured him and his purpose with a fine care. A grizzled old fellow who apparently was not to be bluffed, bullied or stampeded; who stood his ground with a gun on his hip, ready to fight.

How well might he fight? The question flickered behind the banked brutality of Stump Yole's eyes and in High Bob

Caldwell's pinched and now fuming ones. Many an old wolf had made such a stand as this, only to go down because of fangs worn and blunted to uselessness, and physical reactions fatally slowed by the years. Might it be so now?

Stump Yole decided it would and a significant glance passed between him and High Bob.

'Old man,' Yole said, 'you ain't that good. Haul out. I won't tell you again!'

So, suddenly, it was here. And now also, Buck Theodore could look back and see where so many things had been working up to this very moment. Fatalism touched him. He crouched a little lower and threw in all the dice. He went for his gun.

And in one flashing second knew the dismal truth that valor alone was never enough.

Stump Yole did not move, just stared coldly. But High Bob Caldwell moved, and it was like the strike of a snake. Gun report pounded, scattering brief and sullen echoes. Shattering force struck Buck Theodore. It struck him in the chest and knocked him back and down, closing out all his universe in one great thunder-clap of crushing might. Beyond which lay only a deep, deep blackness, thick and without limit.

High Bob Caldwell's horse, spooked by the blare of a gun so close to its head, began to unwind a little but its rider fought it down with savage authority. He slid his gun back into the leather.

'He would have it,' High Bob said, heartless and wickedly cynical.

Stump Yole nodded. 'The damned old fool! Let's get out of here.'

He led the way down the short slope at a run, reined through a covert of willow and sent his horse fording breast-deep water. High Bob Caldwell crowded right at his heels and when they broke into the clear on the far side of the river, spurred up even with his partner.

'There's other camps under the pass, Stump. Scott said to get 'em all.'

'Yeah,' agreed Stump. 'But he didn't say to kill anybody.'

'What the hell!' High Bob blurted. 'You blamin' me? I hadn't stopped him that old feller could have got one of us. He was lookin' right at you.'

'I know he was and I'm not blamin' you,' assured Stump. 'If you hadn't stopped him, I would have. It was just a bum break, that's all.' With some vehemence he said again, 'The damned old fool!'

'You feel so about it, what's the idea anglin' off this way?' asked High Bob.

'Town,' said Stump. 'And fifty dollars. Twenty-five apiece.'

High Bob blinked. 'But the chore ain't finished. And Scott won't pay until—'

'He'll pay unless he gets words of the shootin',' Stump cut in. 'He hears about that, then he could try and stall us. Once I get my twenty-five in my jeans, I don't care what he says or thinks.' He added, with unconscious naivete, 'I just don't trust Tasker Scott.'

High Bob squinted at the morning sky, considering.

'Man can buy a pretty fair whiskey edge on twenty-five dollars,' he murmured presently.

So they rode south toward the town of Antelope, a pair of individuals physically cast in human shape, yet guided almost entirely by primordial brute instincts, and while possessed of a certain degree of animal cunning and courage, lacking totally the better virtues of man.

Up river at the Vail camp, John Vail had recovered enough to take reasonable ease. His two smaller children pressed close to him, previous fears clearing away because of this precious nearness. John Vail smiled at them and caressed them with his hands.

His wife brought him coffee and he was about to take a drink of this when a gun's muffled echo rolled up from the south. Vail cocked his punished head, listening. No further sound came. He looked at his wife, frowning.

'You heard that, Rachel?'

'Yes. A gun. Now why and where—'

200

Kip Vail, tending a pan of sputtering bacon at the fire, straightened. Already sobered by morning's harsh events, she now turned more so.

'That was about where Lee Tracy's camp would be, Father. And those, those two brutes rode that way.'

'Yes,' agreed John Vail. Reading in his daughter's expression a thought to match his own, he put down his coffee cup. 'Maybe I better go take a look.'

'No!' exclaimed Kip quickly. 'I will.'

She was away and gone before he could object.

A swift slender girl, she ran a little, walked a little, then ran again, following the gradual swing of the river, threading close to the fringe of growth bordering it. When she came in view of the camp she sought, she paused, using the shelter of the willows for concealment.

There was a fire burning and a horse stood picketed off to one side, but from this spot Kip could find no one in sight. She pondered this, reaching for its significance. That live fire, more than anything else, decided her. She moved out of the willows and angled up toward the fire. As she climbed past the curve of the slope she saw more than just the fire and the horse. She saw three spreads of blankets, with a saddle lying by one of these. And then there was something else—

something!

She stopped, one slim hand stealing up to her throat. That something was a man, crumpled down close to the earth, huddled as though sleeping. An old man, with shaggy, grizzled hair. But not just sleeping!

Slowly she went closer, close enough to be certain. She saw the spreading stain on the front of a faded shirt. She saw a gun, fallen from lifeless fingers. So now she ran again, back to her father's camp, and she had to reach hungrily for breath, because it was crowded out by the sick emotion catching at her throat.

CHAPTER TWELVE

At Lazy Dollar, Tasker Scott had early breakfast with the crew and gave his orders for the day. First out of the cookshack, Lonnie Raikes had Scott's horse ready. Before stepping into the saddle, Scott carefully lighted the first cigar of the day. Then he swung up and settled himself solidly. He dropped a final order.

'You stay close around, Lonnie. Mrs Scott is not to leave the ranch without my permission. That clear?'

'Clear enough,' Lonnie said in his soft drawl.

Scott held to the town trail for a little time, then cut away to the south. Yesterday he'd made his survey of the upper end of the basin. This morning he would ride through the lower end as far as the river gap. Not only to take first hand measure of the basin's activities and temper, and to renew an overweening sense of possession and authority, but as partial outlet to a simmering restlessness and unsettling frustration which hagged him and filled his thoughts.

In his way he was a precise man, a methodical one, whether the affair at hand be legitimate or otherwise. He liked to lay his plans and then have all parts fall into place accordingly. He had so planned his marriage to Lucy Garland, while reaching beyond this to plot out the advantages and rewards it could bring him. It had seemed for a time that he had planned correctly, but now...

Possession was Tasker Scott's life, and he had thought he possessed Lucy Garland completely. Now he knew that he did not, that he never really had and never really would. Legally she was his. Emotionally she was not, which was more important. And why wasn't she?

Lee Tracy?

Scott ground his teeth and spurred his startled and protesting horse to a run.

Back at the ranch, Lucy Scott, still abed,

203

watched the day grow and brighten outside her window. She had again slept poorly. High strung, tempestuous in her emotions, the present pass come to in her affairs had charged her with a taut explosiveness which denied real rest. She was, she told herself darkly, in a trap of sorts. That was it, a trap. Like some caged animal, fiercely resentful of the bars, but unable to do anything about it.

Or couldn't she? She would do a deal of thinking on it and perhaps come up with an answer. In the meantime, she was through just mooning around the ranchhouse; she was far too vigorous and self-assertive to stand any more of that. Already she had a bad dose of cabin fever. Thoroughly capable in housework when she wished to be, she had been using such to work off some of the edge of restlessness. But there was a limit to that, too. What she needed, she decided, was a brisk spin behind her pet team. Or, better yet, a few hours in the saddle.

It had, she realized with a start, been some time—months in fact—since she had sat in a saddle, having done all her traveling in her buggy. This for two reasons. One because Tasker had wished it so, arguing that it was more dignified and in keeping with her position in life as his wife. The other reason was her own and pretty closely paralleled his. That shining buggy, that spirited, spanking team, had set her apart, made of her a personage. For there was nothing like it in Maacama Basin. In it she was a great lady, apart from all her sex in the basin, which assuaged the ego of an innately selfish woman who was beautiful and rich and who was fully aware of these facts.

But this morning for some reason, the promise of getting into her old riding clothes and seeking the open range away from roads and trails appealed specially. Maybe, she thought wryly, it was another evidence that she, basically, was thoroughly the daughter of her father, with an inherited strain of old Hack Garland's rough and ready character beginning to show through.

In any event, the more she considered the idea the greater its appeal. So, when she rose and dressed, she got into a silk blouse, a divided skirt, and pulled on her old, use-scarred riding boots. She brushed and put up her hair and added a neckerchief for a bit of color at her throat. She had a final look at herself in her big mirror and decided she liked what she saw. It seemed as if she had recaptured a breath of her vanishing girlhood. When she went into the kitchen to stir up a breakfast for herself, she felt lighter of spirit than she had for days.

Lonnie Raikes was puttering at the minor chore of repairing a rail in a corral fence when Lucy came down from the ranchhouse. She had on a white, flat-brimmed Stetson and a buckskin jacket her father had had made up for her, years before. In one hand she carried a pair of gauntlet gloves, in the other a light quirt.

Lonnie straightened from his job, stared a moment, then moved to intercept her as she headed for the saddle shed.

'You aimin' on goin' somewhere, Miz Scott?' he asked, exaggerating his drawl as though in mockery.

Lucy faced him coldly. 'I want you to put my saddle on a good horse.'

Lonnie shook his head. 'Sorry, Miz Scott. That can't be.'

'What do you mean can't be?'

'Your husband's orders. Last thing he said this mornin' before pullin' out; you wasn't to leave the place. That's it, Ma'am.'

Lucy stared as though unable to believe her ears. Then she flared.

'That's ridiculous. I come and go as I please. So get about it. Saddle a horse for me!'

Again Lonnie Raikes shook his head. He had a narrow face, sharp of feature. Above a pointed chin his lips were thin and seemed always about to break into a sneer. His eyes were so pale a blue as to seem almost milky. And they were hard as glass, without any depth. Then there was a faintly rancid odor about the man, as though he'd lain long in his own sweat.

206

Repulsion swelled in Lucy Scott. 'I'll saddle my own horse. Get out of my way!'

She moved to pass him but he was quickly in the doorway of the saddle shed, where he lounged indolently, blocking it.

'Miz Scott, you heard me right the first time,' he murmured. 'You ain't goin' nowhere less'n Mister Scott says so.'

She looked him up and down, hating him, while the spirit of old Hack Garland began to blaze. She gripped her quirt until the knuckles of her hand stood out whitely.

'I'll say it just once more. Get out of my way!'

For a third time Lonnie Raikes shook his narrow head. And Lucy swung her quirt, lashing out at his mocking face. Fast as the blow was, he was faster. He shot up a hand, caught the descending quirt across his open palm, gripped it and with one quick wrench, tore it from Lucy's hand.

'Miz Scott,' he said softly, 'if'n this quirt had landed like you tried, then I reckon I'd have plumb wore it out on you. Best thing you can do is get back to the house and mind your manners before I lose my temper—plumb!'

Past the sense-deadening weight of her own thoroughly awakened fury, Lucy became aware that barely beneath the soft drawling surface of him, this man was all savage, and she knew that as things stood at this moment, she hadn't a chance with him. But that did not mean she was whipped. Far from it!

She gave him one last searing stare, then turned and went back to the ranchhouse, half running.

Lonnie Raikes watched after her, scrubbing the stung palm of his hand up and down on the leg of his jeans. His lips moved, but what they uttered was soundless, of meaning only to some dark depth within him. When Lucy disappeared in the ranchhouse he smiled thinly, tossed the quirt aside and sauntered back to his chore of repairing the corral fence.

In the ranchhouse Lucy sped straight to a room that had been relegated to a sort of storeroom, a catch-all. In a corner several guns were stacked. One of these was a .38-40 Model '92 Winchester, Lucy's own rifle, given to her several years before by her father. With it she had grown proficient enough to bag several deer in the brushy canyon country of the northern Mingo Hills, and in the aspen brakes on Chancellor Peak.

It had been some time since she had fired the gun, but full familiarity returned as she swung the lever back and forth and tested the action. On a nearby shelf was half a box of ammunition. She plugged the fat, stubby cartridges into the loading gate until the magazine was full, then emptied the remainder of the box into her jacket pocket. Then she was once more quickly from the house again, swinging the lever of the rifle to jack a cartridge into the chamber.

Lonnie Raikes was bent over his job, his back to her. He had no idea of her presence until, from a distance of fifty yards she lifted the rifle to her shoulder, took quick sight and sent a bullet slashing into the ground not a yard from his feet. The blunt, hard smash of report, the stinging spatter of dust and the banshee wail of the bullet as it ricocheted from the trampled earth, brought Lonnie up and around in a twisting leap like a startled cat. Hardly had he caught his balance than a second slug ripped a burst of splinters from the corral post beside him. Then Lucy levered home another cartridge and behind the ready threat of this moved up to within twenty feet of him.

'All right, you!' she charged. 'Now we'll see who gives orders on this ranch. Get over there against the saddle shed—quick!'

For a moment Lonnie was too surprised and stunned by it all to move. So that threatening rifle again blasted report and threw the thin acridity of its breath at him along with a bullet that stirred a gout of wind against his face, so closely did it pass. This jarred him loose from his paralysis and sent him at an awkward, scrambling run to the designated spot. He faced the end of the saddle shed, close up.

Chill lay along his spine, for, while he was in no way a complete physical coward, right now there was something about this woman which told him that given sufficient provocation, she would gun him down with no more compunction than if he were a rabid coyote. Full evidence of this showed in the blaze in her eyes, the set of her lips and the hard stridency of her voice as it struck at him again.

'Stay there and don't move! I'm not through with you.'

The shots had rolled their echoes across the headquarters area and the import of them brought the ranch cook to the door of the cookshack. Lucy called to him.

'Get down here, Shad!'

Shad Biggs had been long at Lazy Dollar. He was a stubby little man, mild and colorless and inoffensive, asking nothing more of life than undisturbed tenancy of his cookshack, where he was an undisputed wizard with a skillet or a pot. Now he advanced a little fearfully.

'Whut is it, Lucy?' he asked. Quickly he corrected this. 'Missis Scott, I mean. Whut's wrong? Whut's Lonnie done?'

'Enough,' she told him shortly. 'Catch up a horse and put my saddle on it. And hang a rifle scabbard to the saddle.'

Shad didn't argue. He too, marked the

blaze in Lucy's eyes, judged the set of her chin and that harsh something in her voice which reminded him of old Hack Garland. And Shad could recall clearly the old days when if Hack used that tone it was wise to obey, and quickly!

So now he carried Lucy's riding gear from the shed to the cavvy corral, where he caught up a horse and saddled it. He brought the animal to Lucy and she was swiftly astride, reins in her left hand, while the right held the rifle resting ready against her hip.

'All right, Raikes. You can turn around now!'

He came around slowly, narrow face bloodless, drained by the bitter anger which held him. To be whipsawed by a woman, to have to stand and take it like this from one, crucified what stood for his pride. He showed Lucy a dead, flat stare and appeared to crouch slightly, like an animal about to spring.

She swung her horse near side to him and dropped her rifle across the saddle horn. The muzzle bore fully on him.

'Go ahead, try it!' she taunted. 'Next time I won't just shoot close. I mean that!'

Slowly he dropped back into his usual indolent slouch, reaching for his smoking.

'Yes, Ma'am,' he drawled mechanically, 'I can see you do. So what is it now? You seem to be callin' the turns.'

'You'll start walking,' Lucy said. 'You'll keep on walking until you're completely off Lazy Dollar range. And you'll stay off for good! You can start now!'

The cigarette he'd begun to build dissolved into torn fragments under the sudden stricture of his fingers.

'Ma'am, there's something I reckon you don't fully mean?'

'You're reckoning wrong!' shot back Lucy.

'But my gear, my war-bag in the bunkhouse,' he argued. 'You can't turn me out this way, set me afoot with nothin'. I got a right to—'

'On Lazy Dollar land you haven't a right in the world,' she cut in. 'Start walking!'

He hated her savagely with those pale, dead eyes, while his lips twisted into a soundless curse. He tried to stare her down, but without success. For there was no evidence of softness in her anywhere, no sign of relenting.

'You'll walk now,' she went on remorselessly, 'or you'll never walk again. I'll smash your knees. So help me, I will!'

She brought the rifle to her shoulder. And Lonnie Raikes broke. He cursed again, this time audibly, then whirled and started off.

Lucy sent her horse along after him, and for some distance sat high and taut in her saddle. Then slowly she settled back. Her lips trembled and she blinked angrily as she

212

tried, without too much success to dam up the tears which trickled down her cheeks.

*　　*　　*

What with their early dawn start from the camp, Lee Tracy and Jack Dhu were in town before many people were abroad on the streets of Antelope. The door of Tasker Scott's office was locked, the place empty.

'He'll be along,' Tracy decided. 'We'll wait around. And about now another cup of coffee would go good.'

They sought the eating house across the street and killed the better part of an hour there, dawdling over their coffee and a couple of cigarettes. During this time, Antelope found its true pulse for the day and when they moved out into the street again it was full of growing activity.

They had another look at Scott's office, saw it was still locked, so drifted along to the Trail House. The double doors of this were thrown wide to let out the stale, accumulated odors of last night. Tracy and Jack Dhu turned in here and looked over the scattering of early morning regulars lined at the bar.

One of these was Ben Pardee, and scarce recognizable. He was unshaven, unshorn—frowsy and filthy. His face was bloated, his eyes blurred and rheumy. His mouth was loose and foul and there was a shaky

213

uncertainty in his every move. He was gulping greedily at his liquor, holding the glass in both hands in an effort to steady it. Even so, a full half of the contents spilled down his chin and dribbled along his throat. It was quite plain that he was aware of nothing but the whiskey.

It seemed incredible that over the space of a few short days, liquor or anything else could reduce a man so far from what he had been, a fact which Lee Tracy now remarked.

Jack Dhu studied Pardee a moment, then shrugged.

'Nobody took a club to him and made him go on a bender.'

'I'm not so sure,' Tracy said, his voice low and holding a note of regret. 'Maybe they did, Jack. That physical whipping could have started it, and being made to crawl, after setting out to be a marshal, could have finished the job. A man could set out to drown his shame over something like that. So maybe you and I are responsible and ought to do something about it.'

The lean Texan gave his head a decisive shake.

'Ain't nothing we can do outside hauling him off and tying him up somewhere. Which we ain't about to do. A thing like this has got to run its course. Either he'll end up dead or come through with all his troubles burned out of him. Having been on a couple of benders in my time, I know. Besides, we don't owe him a thing. Remember, he got his licking when he tried to eucher you out of some honestly earned wages. And he ended up crawling when he tried to pull a fake arrest on you, all the time hoping you'd give him just any kind of an excuse to gun you down. No, Lee, you don't owe him a damned thing.'

'Putting it so, I guess I don't,' agreed Tracy reluctantly. 'Yet I can't help feeling sorry for him. After all, for a few days and nights we did eat around the same campfire.'

'Necessity,' Jack Dhu said briefly. 'Not pure choice. Pay him no concern; he's not worth it.'

They went out into the street again and had their look along it. Jack Dhu swung sharply.

'Yonder, Lee! Scott's office.'

Two riders had just pulled up in front of the place and were dismounting. One lank and gangling, the other short and wide, seemingly almost deformed on abnormally short legs.

'That's them,' went on Jack Dhu harshly. 'They're the ones run Buck and me out of the line camp cabin. They had the edge, then. Different, now. Me, I got a few things to say to that pair!'

Stump Yole and High Bob Caldwell. The Texan would have headed for them except for Tracy's restraining hand.

'Later, Jack, later! Scott's the man we came to town to talk to. That pair were just following his orders. We'll get around to them in good time.'

Jack Dhu held his hard stare along the street, reluctant to agree. But he did.

'All right,' he said gruffly. 'Just so we do!'

Watching, Tracy saw Stump Yole try the door of Scott's office, then cup his hands along his temples and peer through a window. After which he turned and made brief comment to his companion. They stood for a little time in seeming indecision, then headed for the Trail House.

'Ah!' exclaimed Jack Dhu. 'We don't have to go after them, they're coming to us.'

'And we're not waiting for them,' Tracy said, his restraining grip on the Texan's arm tightening. 'Our time with those two isn't yet.'

Down street, Asa Bingham was busy at a regular morning chore, that of sweeping off the porch of his store, and it was here that Lee Tracy steered Jack Dhu's reluctant steps. As they climbed the low step, Bingham leaned on his broom and considered them shrewdly. 'You've the look of being up to mischief,' he remarked. 'What?'

'Another talk with Tasker Scott,' Tracy answered. 'But he's not on the job yet.'

216

He and the Texan settled themselves on the bench beside the store door. Up street, Stump Yole and High Bob Caldwell turned in at the Trail House.

Asa Bingham watched a towering freight outfit creak by.

'What kind of talk?'

'A last try to get things settled peaceable.'

'And if it don't work?'

'I guess you know.' There was bleak significance in the words.

'I know,' nodded Bingham slowly. 'And I mortally hate to see it come.' He paused, held for a moment by his thoughts. Then he went on. 'Something I should have told you before. Don't know why I didn't, except the idea of keeping trouble from being stirred up seemed more important just then than anything else. Man can get into a groove of thinking, so, when it seems nothing counts as much as to see things run smooth and quiet, no matter what the price.'

Tracy observed him carefully through a thin drag of cigarette smoke.

'What is this you should have told me, Asa?'

'That mortgage note I sold Tasker Scott. When I drew it up, I wanted to give Buck Theodore plenty of time, so I put a five year call date on it. That was two and a half years ago, maybe a little longer. So the note has at least two more years to run before it can legally be called and a foreclosure instituted.'

A gleam came into Tracy's eyes. 'Then, even though Scott obtained the note by legal means, he had no right to push Buck off Flat T—and wouldn't have for the next two years.'

'That's it,' Bingham said.

'But didn't Buck know about the call date? If he did he's never mentioned it to me.'

'Buck was mighty low when he came to me for the money,' Bingham explained. 'Everything was going wrong for him and he just seemed not to give much of a damn, one way or the other. He never even bothered to read the note. He just signed it. And while I'm not trying to excuse myself for selling the note to Scott, I did figure the five year call date would give Buck time to get squared away again.'

'Of course Scott knew about the call date?'

'Hell, yes!' With equal vehemence, Bingham added: 'That fellow reads both sides of everything, as well as the fine print.'

Jack Dhu, listening, laid an accusing glance on the storekeeper.

'Seein' as you knew all this, why didn't you call Scott on it when he set out to kick Buck off his ranch? Or at least show Buck that he didn't have to get off?'

Dull color burned in Bingham's face.

'That's a question I've asked myself a

thousand times. The only answer I've been able to work out is that I'm just a country storekeeper who's not as young as he used to be, and who's made it a habit to mind his own business for so long, it's a hard one to break. Likewise and besides, the way things were then, Buck was alone and far outnumbered. Somehow it just seemed there was no good to be done by doing anything. So—' He shrugged. 'I'm not proud, understand. I'm just giving it to you straight how it looked to me at the time. I was wrong. So, I was wrong.'

'Put it out of mind, Asa,' soothed Tracy. 'What's done, is done. There were mistakes all around. I made the biggest one, myself. The main thing now is, you've given me another angle to work on Scott. I'll throw that call date at him and watch him squirm.'

Jack Dhu stirred.

'That pair of uglies who been holding down the place? Well, I'm going to take supreme joy in invitin' them to hell off Flat T land and hope they try and argue the point.'

Asa Bingham glanced at him.

'Sure you'll enjoy it. You got the look about you. Like you're ready to dig up hell, then dare the devil to do something about it, should he complain. Wish I could have been that way. But let me tell you something, friend. When you've stood behind a store counter long enough, all the brave juices of

219

life get dried plumb out of you, and you become a timid soul like me.'

Saying which, Bingham swung his broom in a final swipe, then turned back into his store.

CHAPTER THIRTEEN

The morning ran along and the normal business of the town flowed back and forth. Street's dust, churned by hoof and wheel, drifted thinly on the air's idle stirring, and the steadily climbing sun built a heat shimmer across the land until, thickened by distance, it became a haze which seemed to take on an almost palpable substance. In the considerable distance, Chancellor Peak shouldered up in its massive loneliness, blue and remote.

A sudden sweep of feeling came powerfully to Lee Tracy, saying that this was surely his kind of country, this Maacama Basin. Big country, with room enough for everybody, just so everybody was content with his legitimate share and no more. A land in which a man could set his roots deep and find a full life's permanence, and where he could greet each dawn and each sunset with serene content and confidence.

He shifted restlessly under the press of

these thoughts. How easy, he thought ruefully, to muse on the way it could be, and how sobering to face the full reality of the way it was!

'Me, too,' murmured Jack Dhu, stirring beside him. 'When there's something to be done, then just sittin' and waiting is the toughest chore in the world. Now where in hell is Scott? What's holding him up? He don't show pretty quick, I say we go hunt for him. And when we find him, teach him some facts of life.'

Tracy smiled briefly. 'Day's young yet, Jack. He'll show. But I know how you feel.'

The Texan laid his impatient survey along the street. 'And that prize pair in the Trail House. It'd be real interestin' to go tell them off.'

'Perhaps,' Tracy agreed drily. 'But that can wait, too. All things in good time.'

Silence returned. A small, nondescript dog of varied ancestry ambled languidly into view, cast a speculative eye on these two lean, brown-faced men, made tentative advance with the wag of a ragged tail, then sidled up. Tracy rubbed its ears and was repaid for this gesture of fellowship with several licks of a moist pink tongue.

'That proves it,' Jack Dhu declared flatly. 'Some animals got more sense than a lot of humans. Now this little feller didn't know either of us. But being full of the spirit of live and let live, he ambles over, says "Howdy" and makes friends.'

The Texan began twisting up another smoke, his restless glance roaming. It reached further down street toward the edge of town and there saw something to turn him momentarily still and wondering. After which he exclaimed.

'Be damned! If that's not Buck Theodore's horse, then I never laid eyes on the bronc before. And it's the granger girl, the Vail girl, who's in the saddle!'

Tracy had been leaning forward, petting the dog. Jack Dhu's words brought him up, straight and staring.

Kip Vail had apparently just turned into town, and there was no doubt about the horse she was riding. Tracy hit his feet and moved to the edge of the porch. At his elbow, Jack Dhu made further observation.

'From the way she keeps swinging her head, that girl's lookin' for somebody. Wonder could it be us?'

Tracy dropped into the street and headed toward her. Tossing away his forgotten cigarette, the Texan followed.

She saw them immediately and rode sharply forward, stopping just as sharply, looking down with a great and sober relief.

'I had hoped to—to find you.' The tone was ragged, the words faltering.

Her fair hair was loose and wind-blown

across her shoulders and her eyes were big and dark, holding something that stirred the bleakest of premonitions in Lee Tracy.

'What is it, Kip?'

She slipped from the saddle before answering.

'The old man in your camp—'

'Buck!' exclaimed Tracy. 'Buck Theodore. Something's wrong with him?'

She nodded, plainly reluctant to give out all the word.

Premonition closed down tighter on Tracy. And somehow, suddenly, he knew.

'He's dead?'

'Y-yes.' The word broke slightly. 'Somebody—shot him!'

Jack Dhu made a strange sound deep in his throat, an eruptive sound, half growl, half snarl.

'Who?' he burst out. 'Girl, who did it?'

'I can't say for positive. But I think, I think—' Again she faltered, reaction setting in.

'You think who?' insisted Jack Dhu.

'Easy, Jack,' Tracy cautioned. 'We need the full straight of this. You look after the horse. Kip, this way.'

He took her arm and guided her into Asa Bingham's store and over to a far corner where a small, railed off enclosure held a couple of chairs and Bingham's old, roll-top desk with its burden of ledgers and catalogues and order books. Bingham, arranging some stock, threw a questioning glance.

Tracy said, 'It's all right, Asa.'

He brought one of the chairs forward for Kip Vail, then stood beside her and spoke gently.

'Take your time and tell it all.'

She drew several deep breaths, which appeared to steady and quiet her.

'They came into our camp. There were two of them. They were rough and brutal. They told my father he had to pack up and move along, that we were on another man's land. Dad said we were not and that he refused to move. So one of them tried to ride him down. There was a struggle and Dad was hit on the head with a gun. They rode on, then, down river, saying they'd be back that way and that we'd better not be there when they did.'

'You said there were two of them,' prompted Tracy. 'What did they look like? And did they drop any names?'

She thought for a moment. She was much steadier, now, more sure of herself.

'One was tall and thin and the other just the opposite, short and thick. And this one called the tall one Bob.'

'Of course,' murmured Tracy grimly. 'They would be the ones.'

'Yeah,' rapped Jack Dhu, who had come

224

in to listen, striding high and harsh. 'Yeah—that pair. And we know where they are, right now! Let's do something about it!'

'Presently,' said Tracy. 'There's more to this. Kip, you say that when they left your camp they headed down stream?'

She nodded. 'In the direction of your camp. After a little time a shot sounded. Dad and I wondered. So, presently, I went to see. The old man was lying there dead. He'd been shot. He must have tried to shoot back, because a gun lay near his hand.'

'Sure,' ground out Jack Dhu savagely. 'That's how they'd work it. Rawhide the old feller into tryin', all the time knowin' his years had slowed him to where he didn't have a chance. Lee, what we waiting for?'

'The rest of it.' Tracy touched Kip on the shoulder. 'There was nobody around our camp but Buck?'

'Just, just him. But those riders had been there. After I'd taken the word back to Dad and Mother and we'd decided what to do—which was that I'd take the old man's horse and try and find you—I started to think better. So I followed the tracks of the two riders, straight to your camp. I followed them away from your camp. They crossed the river and turned south toward town, but after a bit the trail mixed up with a lot of other tracks so I couldn't be sure just where they led.'

'We know,' Jack Dhu growled. 'We know!'

'Yes,' nodded Tracy somberly, 'we know.' He touched her shoulder again. 'Thanks, Kip, thanks!'

She came to her feet. 'What are you going to do?'

He paused, brooding, then said carefully, 'Something I should have done in the first place.'

'Dad's set to fight if those men come back,' reminded Kip a little desperately. 'He vowed he would—with his old buffalo gun. And there's Mother and the two little ones—'

'They won't come back, that pair,' Tracy told her. He turned away then and Jack Dhu fell in beside him.

While Tracy and the Texan had been listening to Kip Vail's story, two different arrivals moved into town. The first of these was Lonnie Raikes, limping on badly blistered feet, heading straight for the Trail House and the solace of whiskey. A short minute before Lonnie's arrival Stump Yole and High Bob Caldwell, riding the crest of several whiskies of their own, had left the Trail House for another look into Tasker Scott's office. They were at the door of this when Scott himself rode up and dismounted.

He gave them a quick, hard scrutiny. 'What are you two doing here?'

'Told you we'd be by to collect, didn't

we?' Stump Yole reminded.

'You couldn't have finished that chore already,' charged Scott.

'It's finished,' said Yole glibly. 'Bob and me, we don't fool around. When we tell grangers to move on, they move!'

Scott, not fully convinced, considered a moment. 'All the camps weren't grangers. One in particular. How about that one?'

Stump Yole's heavy lids drooped slightly.

'Only an old feller there. He didn't argue—much.'

Again Scott hesitated. Knowing the untrustworthiness of his own words and purposes, he was cynical of all other men and their motives. However, here there was no other answer visible but the apparent one, so he shrugged and unlocked the office door.

On leaving Asa Bingham's store, Lee Tracy and Jack Dhu went along to the Trail House. Lee Tracy was held by the strangest feeling he had ever known. It was a peculiar inner stillness, as though in some queer way he now stood beyond the limits of strictly ordered thought, and was functioning instead under the guidance of a smooth and effortless reflex which was pointing him toward a destiny he could neither avoid or deny.

Initial word of Buck Theodore's death had been a wrenching jolt to numb him beyond immediate pain; the pain would come later.

Just now he moved through an area of detachment, like some puppet answering a primal instinct, rather than considered reason.

Jack Dhu spoke, cold and quiet.

'Don't pack any fancy ideas into a deal like this, Lee. You'll be meeting with a breed that deserve nothing, no even shake, no nothing! Long side of them a rattlesnake is a gentleman; he at least will give warning before he strikes. Not so with this pair. You show one breath of weakness with them and they'll kill you. Believe me, I know!'

At the Trail House the Texan pushed in ahead, gaunt and hawkish, his glance searching swiftly. Not finding those he wanted, he turned to the bartender.

'Two fellers who were in here a little bit ago? One tall like me. The other short and with stubby legs like a bear. Where'd they go?'

'Couldn't say,' shrugged the bartender. 'They just left a couple of minutes from now. I heard one of them say something about an office.'

'Obliged,' said Jack Dhu, wheeling back to the door. 'You heard, Lee? An office. That means Scott's.'

Standing in the doorway of the land office, Rufe Wilkens had noted Tasker Scott's arrival and short trading of words with Stump Yole and High Bob Caldwell before leading the way inside. Now it was Lee Tracy and Jack Dhu who came by, striding purposefully toward the same destination, apparently—and with something about them to give any shrewd man reason for pause. Rufe Wilkens was shrewd enough, and wary, too—ever one to take note of such signs and to dredge up the meaning behind them. So he remained as he was, waiting and watchful.

In his office, Tasker Scott moved to the chair behind the desk. Stump Yole, pressing a fancied advantage, hooked a heavy hip on a desk corner and lounged so, swinging his foot. High Bob Caldwell, like some gaunt and wary dog suspicious of the confinement of any four walls and what might lie within them, stood apart, his glance darting and watchful.

Scott missed neither of these attitudes and was irked by both. Again he knew sharp resentment and distaste over circumstances that forced him to deal with such men as these. They were offensive to both eye and nostril, ugly and dirty all the way through. Yet there was a certain competency about them which made it plain they never fully accepted the authority of any man.

Scott knew they tolerated him and his orders on the promise of immediate creature rewards and for no other reason. What little control you might hold over them, you bought. Once you ceased to buy them they were no longer your men. They were like feral animals that would jump through a hoop for the promise of food. Deny them that and they would turn on you with tooth and claw.

'You had to move fast to touch all the camps under the pass,' said Scott, still skeptical.

'And I say again that grangers don't argue with Bob and me,' Stump Yole retorted. 'When we say move, they move!'

'That other camp?' probed Scott. 'Only an old fellow was there?'

'That's all.'

'And he didn't put up any argument?'

Stump Yole hesitated ever so slightly. 'Not much of a one.'

'That would have been Buck Theodore,' Scott observed. 'And even if he argued only a little, you had to do something to convince him. What did you do?'

Again Stump showed that bare moment of hesitation.

'We just made up his mind for him.'

'How?'

When, as now, there was a whiskey edge in High Bob Caldwell, there was little time left for the trading of words. Words confused his small, cold brain, and having to fence with them made him uncertain and impatient and irritable. And while generally one to let his partner do the talking for both of them, there was a limit to patience that swiftly wore wire-thin. Such limit was now reached and he burst out viciously.

'I took care of him!'

'Care of him?' Scott reared forward in his chair. 'You didn't kill him?'

'I damn well did!' droned High Bob nasally. 'He tried for his gun, and any time anybody goes to throw a gun on Stump or me, they better be able to finish the ride!'

'We expect to finish this one, Caldwell!' The words came from the office doorway. Lee Tracy spoke them harshly, as he and Jack Dhu stepped quickly through.

Surprise complete, froze Tasker Scott.

Not so High Bob and Stump Yole. Old in the wicked experience of this sort of thing, both instantly understood the challenge and the deadly need.

Stump Yole slid from the desk, coming square around. High Bob Caldwell whirled in flashing movement. But he wasn't out-matching Buck Theodore's age-hampered reflexes this time. In Jack Dhu he was trying against his full equal and better. And so High Bob was not quite there when the Texan's gun charged the room with the chopping blast of report. High Bob Caldwell's head jerked back and all of life's substance immediately left him. He crumpled to the floor, fully dead before he reached it.

Hardly had the echoes of the Texan's shot begun to roll than they were caught up and partially smothered by the smash of Tracy's gun. Tracy had no conscious realization of drawing and shooting, yet there the gun was in his hand, bouncing with recoil. And Stump Yole, hard hit, was staggering. But he showed no sign of going down, and Tracy shot again. A second time that squat, thick figure lurched, yet still stayed upright on those short, spraddled legs.

Now, finally, Stump got off a shot of his own, but by this time all his coordination had been knocked askew, so the slug flew high and wild, thudding into the wall above the door. Committed and remorseless, Tracy threw a third shot and this one set off a blood-chilling craziness in Stump Yole.

Sound broke from his heavy, peeled-back lips, sound that was more the bawl of a mortally wounded animal than it was any human expression. And while uttering it, Stump reeled and stumbled and finally spun completely around, all the while throwing shot after shot, blindly and with no clear purpose.

Beyond his desk, Tasker Scott, for the first few crashing moments, had held still, stunned with the surprise of the thing. Then came the desperate understanding that right here and now was either the complete end of an old trail, or the possibility to start a new one. And it was strictly up to him to try and make it the latter. He hauled the gun from his coat pocket and started up, wholly intent on Lee Tracy.

He was partially out of his chair when Stump Yole, coming around in that final crazy whirl, turned loose a last shot, before falling blind and dying half across the desk. That last chance bullet took Tasker Scott squarely in the center of the throat, knocking him back into his chair, which then over-turned with a shattering crash.

Stump Yole, ponderous and loose, began to slide, his spread, clawing fingers dragging—dragging to the edge of the desk and off it. Then he was fully on the floor, stubby legs twisting, boot-heels drumming. Abruptly movement ceased, and sound, too. Though it came to Lee Tracy that the pounding voices of wild guns would forever echo in his battered consciousness.

Jack Dhu, staring down at Stump Yole, exclaimed.

'How hard can a man die? He was a regular bear who walked like a man!'

Tracy made no answer, but moved past the desk for a look at Tasker Scott. Who lay on his back, arms flung wide, one leg straight, one hooked over the seat of the upset chair. Wide open eyes, staring at the ceiling, were sightless.

Tracy turned away and Jack Dhu followed

him out into the street, where several people, drawn by the sudden rumble of gunfire, were converging on the office. One was Asa Bingham. Another was the land agent, Rufe Wilkens. Then there was Lonnie Raikes and some others from the Trail House. Also came a lone mule skinner and half a dozen curious grangers.

Tracy faced them, looked them over and spoke with a spare bluntness.

'There are three dead men in there. One is Tasker Scott. The other two were his men, acting under his orders. This morning that pair killed my partner, Buck Theodore, an old man who had no chance against them. So they were called to account. In the ruckus one of them, shooting blind and wild, killed Tasker Scott by mistake. Which is not offered as an excuse; it just happens to be the truth. But if that chance shot hadn't killed Scott, one of mine would have. For I went in there after him. Now you know!'

Asa Bingham was still panting from his run. Yet he was a mild man suddenly turned stern and purposeful, who moved up beside Tracy and Jack Dhu, faced the crowd and had his say.

'Most of you know me; at one time or another you've been in my store. I've been in this town a long time. I saw its beginnings. I helped build it and hold it together. Men who know me well know that my reputation and my word are good. So, the day when duly constituted and honestly served law comes to Maacama Basin, I will back and solidly support it. In the meantime, I will personally vouch for these men. What they did, they were honor bound to do. I say again—I vouch for them. Would anyone deny me that right?'

No one spoke up to do so. Bingham identified a man with a nod.

'Tim Asher, take charge of things here. Don't let anyone inside. I will get some proper men together and we will handle the matter with proper consideration for all concerned. Is that satisfactory, gentlemen?'

His glance canvassed the crowd. There were no objectors. For this was still wild country where men had to stand or fall by the measure of their own acts. The crowd began drifting away.

Lonnie Raikes limped back to the Trail House, seeing nothing in his future now but a move into new country. For with Tasker Scott dead, there was no chance of ever getting back on at Lazy Dollar.

Returning to the land office, Rufe Wilkens's face was dark. Mark Kenna met him at the door, questioning.

'What happened?'

'What happened!' Wilkens shrugged. 'Thunder and lightning and a large sized chunk of distilled hell. Which wiped out any

235

hope you and I had of finding something worthwhile in this cursed basin. From now on, we are strictly what we were when we came here, and strictly what we'll be when we leave.'

'Scott,' blurted Kenna. 'How about him? He promised—'

'Scott's dead,' Wilkens cut in savagely. 'Dead and be damned to him! He went and got himself killed. Thereby pulling the big joke on us.'

Harshly laughing, Rufe Wilkens went on into the back office where a whiskey bottle waited.

CHAPTER FOURTEEN

They buried Buck Theodore at sundown, close to the base of the Chancellor Peak escarpment. They laid his head to the east, his feet to the west. It was simply done. Asa Bingham came out from town in a buckboard. Kip Vail and her father were there, having driven across the basin in their big camp wagon. At the last moment a flashing buggy behind a spanking team of matched bay horses came speeding, with Lucy Scott, dressed in dark, sober gray, stepped carefully down.

Her face composed, her eyes shadowed,

she stood apart with bowed head, remaining so while Jack Dhu and John Vail mounded up the grave. Lee Tracy went over to her.

'It was good of you to come, Lucy,' he told her gravely. 'Under the circumstances I thought—'

'Yes,' she interrupted quickly, 'I knew what you would think. But I'm not that callous, Lee. After all, Tasker was my husband, and we did find some good moments I shall probably recall and weep over, later. He will be buried tomorrow, and I wish it to be with some dignity. Which would be impossible if he went to his grave a thief. So I've come to do what I can to wipe out that stain. Might we—step into the house?'

'Of course.'

Earlier in the afternoon a couple of hours had been put in cleaning up the worst of the mess of careless living that Stump Yole and High Bob Caldwell had left behind them in the Flat T ranchhouse, so the room Tracy ushered Lucy into was not too bad. There he turned and faced her, waiting.

She drew two folded papers from the throat of her dress, she handed them to him, explaining.

'This one is the mortgage note Tasker bought from Asa Bingham. Tear it up.'

'Tear it up?' Tracy exclaimed. 'No! Because it represents a legitimate debt which

237

I intend to have paid off by the time the call date comes due.'

'Tear it up!' Lucy insisted. 'If you don't, I shall. The other paper is my authorization for you to select three hundred head of Lazy Dollar white-faces, vent them to your brand and put them on your own range. I have fired most of my crew except Joe Roach and a couple of others I know are honest and who I can trust. I've told Joe about this authorization and he stands ready to help you with the stock. Lee, am I being fair? I know I can't make it up to you for everything. But so far as I can, I'm trying.'

'You're being very fair,' he told her quietly. 'And I think, right now, I admire you more than I ever truly did before.'

She stiffened, staring at him across the room's gloom, startled, and half-eagerly wondering. But what she thought, or perhaps hoped she might see, was not there. He was merely a grave and distant man who had spoken a simple opinion that was completely objective and matter-of-fact, holding no semblance of a deeper sentiment.

Her head dropped again.

'I'm glad, Lee. I would always want your good opinion. I'm leaving Maacama Basin for a while. A few weeks, perhaps a month or two. Joe Roach will be in charge at Lazy Dollar. See him when you get ready to start with the cattle. And to you, Lee—in all things—good luck!'

She went out and away then, quickly. From the ranchhouse doorway Tracy watched her buggy speed off. Then, abruptly, he realized that John Vail's big wagon was also rolling across the flats. Only Asa Bingham was left, trading a few final words with Jack Dhu. Tracy crossed to them.

'Stick around for supper, Asa.'

Bingham shook his head. 'Thanks, I got to get back. That store of mine is a demanding mistress. You'll be staying here on Flat T now, Lee?'

'That's right. Both of us—Jack and me. As full partners.'

When the buckboard rattled off, Jack Dhu turned to Tracy, drawling.

'What was that you just said about you and me being partners?'

'A fact,' affirmed Tracy. 'Half of this ranch and what it becomes in the future is yours, Jack. I know old Buck would have liked it that way. I do, too.'

'It's an idea I'll have to get used to,' said the Texan, softly.

Tracy, considering the matter settled, stared across the flats at the receding bulk of the big Vail wagon, now merging into the deepening shadows.

'They didn't have to move out so quick,' he grumbled. 'What the devil got into them?'

Jack Dhu smiled meagerly. 'From where I stood, I'd say it was because the girl was a mite upset. I know when she told her pa they were leaving, there was something in her voice that sure convinced him. He never argued none.'

'Not like Kip to lose her nerve after all she's been through,' Tracy declared.

'I never said she lost her nerve,' corrected the Texan. 'I just suggested that probably her pretty nose was out of joint. Because you kind of walked away and left her standing there, didn't you? While you escorted another mighty good-looking woman into your house. What did you expect?'

They cooked and ate supper, Tracy grave and restless, Jack Dhu shielding himself behind obscure thoughts of his own. Outside, the night wind began slipping down from old Chancellor, bringing the chill breath of the lonely heights. Tracy pulled on a coat.

'Going for a little jaunt, Jack.'

'Sure, boy, sure,' acknowledged the Texan.

He listened to the departing hoof-drum of Lee's quick jogging horse. After which he began gathering up his few possessions. He went outside and saddled up. At the creek he cut a couple of well-leafed willow branches and laid them, crossed, on the ranchhouse door step.

'You'll know what that sign means,' he murmured. 'That this camp is empty and open to your next partner. Who'll be that pretty little granger girl you're off to visit with. Yeah, you'll be bringing her home one of these days to set up housekeeping. When that happens, I'll be in the way. So it's best I shake loose now, while the going is easier. Come morning, I'll be far from here.'

*   *   *

At the Vail camp, things were subdued. The younger children were in bed. John Vail and his wife sat beside their campfire, used to such quiet hours together by the open flames, and content in their silent understanding.

Lee Tracy sent forward a quiet call before riding up and dismounting.

'You didn't wait for me to thank you for everything,' he told John Vail gruffly. 'So I do, now.'

But even as he spoke, his glance was searching here and there impatiently.

Past her gentlest, wisest smile, Rachel Vail said, 'She went after another bucket of water, Lee.'

He went down into the deep night shadows by the river and never saw her until she spoke.

'Aren't you riding in the wrong direction,

241

Mister Tracy? The lovely Mrs Scott isn't anywhere around here.'

He turned, and by the thin gleam of starlight, discovered her sitting quietly on a low gravel bank. He moved toward her.

'Be still,' he ordered gruffly. 'I'm not interested in anybody but you.'

'How nice,' she jeered. 'So finally he gets around to me. I wonder why?'

'You know why. Nobody else counts. I want to take you home with me.'

'Goodness gracious!' There was a short, breathless pause. Then, a trifle faintly, 'I'm afraid the small question of marriage must be taken care of before that can happen.'

'Tomorrow,' Tracy said. 'There's bound to be a sky pilot in this basin somewhere. Tomorrow we hunt him up.'

She laughed now, and softly. 'You needn't sound so fierce about it. Come sit by me and tell me more...'

L. P. Holmes was born in a snowed-in log cabin in the heart of the Rockies near Breckenridge, Colorado in 1895. For his first story, *The Passing of the Ghost*, Holmes was paid ¢½ per word. He went on to contribute nearly 600 stories to the magazine market, as well as to write over fifty Western novels under his own name and Matt Stuart. Holmes's Golden Age as an author was from 1948 to 1960. During these years he produced such notable novels as *Desert Range*, *Black Sage*, *Summer Range*, *Dead Man's Saddle*, and *Somewhere They Die*, for which he received the Golden Spur Award from the Western Writers of America.